T0209147

.

A Psalm for Sonia

Martín Anderson

A PSALM FOR SONIA

iUniverse books may be ordered through booksellers or by contacting:

iUniverse
1663 Liberty Drive
Bloomington, IN 47403
www.iuniverse.com
844-349-9409

ISBN: 978-1-6632-5992-9 (sc)
ISBN: 978-1-6632-5993-6 (e)

Library of Congress Control Number: 2024901059

Print information available on the last page.

iUniverse rev. date: 02/22/2024

For Marina
and
The Puerto Rican Diaspora

CHAPTER 1

*T*hree loud shots that sounded like cannons came from inside the auto body shop. Within minutes the sound of sirens penetrated the peaceful Sunday morning in April. Even before Sonia Concepción completely woke up, she knew that all of this commotion had probably been caused by a dice game having gone wrong in the auto mechanic shop two buildings up the street, and that more than likely the owner Angel Cintron also known as 'Big Angel,'was involved. For nothing, absolutely nothing went on in his establishment without his permission.

Sonia had moved to this neighborhood about ten years ago and really loved it. Her son Miguel Angel and daughter Marisol were 10 and 9 years old at the time. The subway station that took her downtown to work was only a block away. Miguel Angel made friends at the local park, which was for some children a magical place. On summer afternoons girls and boys between the ages of 8 to 13 could be found at the pool, swimming, diving and holding their breath, counting how long they could stay underwater. The thick glass exterior doors of the pool would be rolled open, converting it into a huge urban lake. Water splashed high in every direction, and the joyful sounds of children calling each other and laughing loudly could be heard by the people trying to read at the public library across the street.

In the winter with the below zero temperatures, howling wind, and snow it was a completely different story. Only a few of the children could be found in trunks swimming as fast as they could. Miguel Angel was one of them. He could not wait for the school dismissal bell to ring at 2:30 so that he could walk, almost run, there. Diving from the board on the high platform gave him a rush that he did not receive anywhere else. What had started off as a dare in which he was scared out of his mind had become an activity that gave him a tremendous sense of pride and accomplishment. He became an excellent diver who could twist and contort his body while performing somersaults in mid air. Here he did not have to feel the sting of being ridiculed and laughed at, which was an almost every day occurrence at school. No matter how hard he tried to focus, he could not make sense of the lines, dots and circles that were suppose to make letters representing sounds. Yes, here on the diving board he was free to fly into the sky with his arms outstretched.

After each dive his friends yelled; "Man that was a bad dive Miguel."

This pool was an enchanting oasis for Miguel Angel. His mother Sonia came here for diving meets to cheer him on. As opposed to defending him against a school system, in which he found almost no happiness and needed his mother to constantly stand up for him.

On one occasion when Miguel was in fifth grade she was summoned into the principal's office after an incredibly frustrated Miguel Angel had thrown a book in class. During Social Studies Miguel had his book closed and the teacher called on him to read a passage about the first Thanksgiving. Miguel saw a boy poke a distracted student while pointing at Miguel with a big smile on his face, getting ready to laugh. Miguel started reading and stumbled helplessly over the word forest.

"That isn't funny children", said Mrs. Patterson.

In a split second Miguel Angel picked up the heavy book and hurled it over Mrs. Patterson's head and it made a loud thud when it hit the chalk board. Sonia was called in to meet with the principal the following day.

"Thank you for coming today Mrs. Candelaria. Hopefully we can correct whatever is wrong with Miguel Angel" said the principal Mr. Mulholland.

Sonia looked up at the clock next to the huge American flag. Mr. Mulholland was sitting right in front of it. To his right was the assistant principal Mr. Carson, who only smiled after telling parents that their child had to serve detention, be suspended or receive some other kind of punishment for their bad behavior. The man to the left of the principal was the counselor Bradley Young. His blue jeans and boots, along with his long hair and his willingness to to tell Sonia that Miguel was a respectful child, helped put her at ease.

"As I was saying Mrs. Candelaria," Mr. Mulholland continued.

"Ms. Concepción," she corrected him.

"I'm sorry?" said Mr. Mulholland.

"It is Ms. Concepción, my name."

"Ok..... Miguel Angel is a big disruption in class and has difficulty following orders, I mean instructions, given by the teacher."

Sonia looked at the clock again, thinking about her job interview for the secretarial position at the trade school. If she could get out of the school by 8:30 it would give her enough time to catch the Chicago Ave. bus downtown. Thoughts about the increase in pay, and more importantly, the opportunity to use her mind more creatively and leave the assembly line behind beckoned.

"Ms. Concepción I notice that you keep looking at the clock. Isn't this important to you?" asked Mr. Mulholland.

"Maybe she has an appointment" interjected Mr. Young.

Sonia smiled and thanked Bradley Young letting him know that he was correct. Then she continued to plead her case.

"I spoke with my son and he was very sorry for throwing the book against the wall. I told him that he must apologize to his teacher."

"That's good but we can't go on letting Miguel break the rules. He has to serve a suspension and this can't happen again" said Mr. Carson, while smiling.

"Don't worry, it won't. But I need for him to be in school. I can't have him at home by himself."

Sonia's real concern was that she knew Miguel Angel would not stay home if he was suspended. He would make his way downstairs, out the door and up the street to Big Angel's auto shop.

"Rules are rules," said Mr. Carson.

"Yes and I appreciate your rules for my son, but I need him here, in school. There must be something else that he can do."

"He threw a book and could have hurt a child Ms. Concepción" said Mr. Carson.

"Reading is hard for my boy. I sit and read with him every night. He tries and tries but saying the words isn't easy for him.

He is doing his best. Please. My daughter also helps him. He can't be suspended, I need him here in school and not at home by himself. Don't you understand?" Sonia looked Mr. Mulholland squarely in the eyes sitting up straight in her chair with her hands folded in front of her.

Mr. Young offered a compromise. Miguel Angel would be technically suspended from school but he would spend the day with Mr. Young as his assistant.

Mr. Mulholland accepted, and Mr. Carson was a bit dejected but went along with it and Sonia thanked them all before leaving the school and catching the bus to her job interview.

Sonia had won the battle that day but ultimately she could not keep her son away from Big Angel. Miguel would only feel the exhilaration and sense of purpose that he did while on the diving board, when he discovered his incredible abilities as an auto mechanic. Miguel learned as a result of Big Angel letting him play with and explore old worn out motors. After learning all he could on parts that were taken out of cars he began asking the mechanics a series of unending questions as they worked. His curiosity started becoming a bit of a nuisance.

"Hey Angel, is that kid gonna be here today? I gotta finish replacing the alternator on that '74 Mustang." Asked José as he walked pass Big Angel's office.

"What kid?", answered Big Angel.

"Come on man you know who I'm talkin' about. He's the only one here askin' questions all day."

"Miguel Angel?"

"That's the one!"

Big Angel was sitting at his desk and reading the Sun Times sports section and lowered the paper just enough to make eye contact. "Listen. Let me tell you, Miguel is welcome here anytime every day of the week. Got a problem with that?"

"Got it Big Angel. No problem at all."

In addition to the pool and library, another special part of the neighborhood was the Polish bakery. It was a remnant of the former residents as most of them had left to live further north, making room for the new Puerto Rican and later Mexican immigrants. It opened at six in the morning and Sonia would send her daughter Marisol for fresh Kaiser rolls and chocolate long johns. This breakfast treat softened the morning rush.

Initially Marisol hated walking to the bakery for the morning sweets. She was extremely shy, and it pained her to ask for anything. She would take a number and would dread when her turn to be served came around. The owner Helen, from behind the counter would have to ask her three times to please speak up.

However, with time Marisol became enamored with the little space. The fresh smell of freshly baked bread combined with the different languages and accents that could be heard had an intoxicating effect on her. The women who worked there often spoke to each other in Polish while the customers spoke to each other in Spanish and then ordered in English. Most children would have taken this for granted but not Marisol. It was difficult for her to talk about this so she kept her thoughts and feelings in her journal.

With the passing of time Marisol eventually found a job that fit her personality perfectly at the greenhouse up the street from their home. In this comforting space she could lovingly tend to the plants and flowers without the burden of having to talk to people all day.

Their apartment was located on the second floor, above a tavern. Surprisingly enough it was pretty quiet. Most of the customers were older men who went in after working their shift at a factory to have their whiskey shots followed by a beer. Occasionally they would argue about the Cubs or Sox being a better baseball team but for the most part they sat on their stools and drank while exchanging friendly banter.

Some of Sonia's friends thought that she was crazy for moving to this apartment with Miguel Angel and Marisol. But after the death of their father Rafael, in her mind she had very little choice. The rent was more than reasonable and Miguel Angel and Marisol would not have to be moved to another school.

Sonia weighed all of these practical concerns but even more important for her was moving to a place that did not carry memories of Miguel Angel and Marisol's father, Rafael Candelaria. They had met at a family picnic in the summer, introduced by Dolores, a friend they had in common.

Rafael was a soft - spoken man who managed a local movie theatre. He only drank on weekends and occasionally would accompany his friends to the racetrack. One day out of curiosity he decided to bet on a horse that according to his friends was a sure bet to win.

From the moment the race began Rafael immediately noticed the difference in his level of interest and most of all excitement. The bell rang and the horses bolted out of the gate! The pounding sound of the horses galloping at high speeds was muffled by the loud cheering of the people shouting encouragement.

"Come on Crimson! Come on!" shouted a couple that was standing next to Rafael.

An older man in a fedora and chomping on the remnants of a cigar angrily cried out; "Come on Pirate you son of a bitch, I got five K on you!"

Rafael's eyes almost popped out of his head when he saw that his horse Louisville Slugger, was about to win the race.

"I won! I won!" he shouted, while jumping up and down and hugging his friend Justino.

As time went on, these victories came few and far between. The losses started mounting and the gambling debts kept adding up. He always paid them, but there was no doubt that he was hooked. Yet as far gone as he was he never displayed any anger with Miguel Angel and Marisol whom he loved unconditionally.

One night he came home and started to ask Sonia for $20 to bet on a new horse, 'The Great Galloper.'

"No! I said no! Rafael we need this money for the rest of the week" said Sonia.

"But, Junito said that this horse can't lose" said Rafael trying to convince her.

"Then get the money from Junito."

"Why are you being like this?"

"Me? Stop this craziness! That's it! No more!"

They were in the kitchen and Sonia turned her back to him and continued stirring the rice on the stove. She saw a desperate look in his eyes and it frightened her. Miguel Angel was in the adjacent room watching Alfalfa sing to Darla on the *Our Gang* TV reruns.

Rafael walked closer to Sonia. "What, you're the man here now? You say how we spend money?"

"Can't you see me cooking? Do I look like the man of the house?" answered Sonia. She knew that in his present state, having his manhood challenged would take Rafael over the edge.

"Then give me the money right now!" Rafael said, stomping his right foot down on the linoleum floor.

"I can't. Last week I gave you $60, and the week before that $40, all of it for betting and losing on those stupid ra———"

"Shut up! You're going to give me that money!"

Rafael started walking in a calculated fury and picked up a baseball bat on the way to where Miguel Angel was watching TV. Sonia followed him.

Rafael held the bat in his hand and turned to Sonia. "Do I make like Clemente or do you give me the..?"

"No!" Sonia held firm.

Miguel Angel saw his father raise the bat and screamed at him begging him to stop. "Pop n———"

Before Miguel Angel could finish screaming no, the television screen had a huge hole in the middle and the jagged lines came out from the center.

"Stop it! You're sick! Here take it!" yelled Sonia, as she threw her purse at Rafael.

He went through it taking out what ever bills he could find and walked out of the front door, slamming it on his way out of the apartment.

Miguel just sat in front of the TV shaking and crying. Sonia held him in her arms rocking and comforting him. "Betting on those horses has made your father lose his mind. He doesn't know what he's doing, son."

Marisol was in her room and decided to come out, feeling safe now that her father was gone. She could not believe that she had heard him in such a rage. When she made it to Sonia and Miguel the only thing she could think of doing was wrapping her arms around both of them. "I love you mami and Migue."

They stayed that way for a few minutes in the silence created by Rafael's irrational blind anger. Then Sonia said; "You both must be hungry. Let's eat."

Sonia saw that Marisol got a broom and started cleaning the broken glass.

"Miguel Angel please help your sister, while I get everything ready."

When the three were at the table Miguel Angel grabbed his fork and started eating his arroz con gandules. Sonia gently tapped him on the shoulder and said, "We pray first." It seemed strange to Marisol that her mother would even want to pray and give thanks after what had just happened, but she said grace and didn't question Sonia.

Later that night while all three were sleeping the phone rang at 2 AM. Sonia picked it up after 5 rings, each one louder than the one before.

"Huhhh, hello?"

"Yes. Mrs. Candelaria?" Said the man on the other end of the line.

"No, Ms. Concepción." Sonia looked at the clock on her nightstand and couldn't believe that someone was calling at this time.

"You must be looking for Mr. Candelaria," said Sonia.

"No ma'am. Are you related to Mr. Rafael Candelaria?"

"Yes. He is the father of my children." Rafael was so much more than that but it was not the time to explain that they were not officially married.

"Well, Ms. a, a,"

"Concepción!" Snapped a tired Sonia.

"I am so sorry ma'am but I am Sergeant Wilson from the police department. I regret to inform you that Mr. Candelaria is dead ma'm. He died in a car accident."

A few weeks after the most tumultuous night of her life is when Sonia made the decision to leave this place and find a new neighborhood and home for her and her children.

CHAPTER 2

*T*en years had passed since the night that Sonia received that dreadful phone call. And after hearing the shots being fired on this Sunday morning, Sonia went to church. She did not bother to wake Miguel Angel or Marisol as she did not feel ready to have that battle of convincing them to accompany her. Instead she enjoyed a bowl of corn flakes and a glass of orange juice, then she got ready to go and pray to God for the right words to move Big Angel's heart.

The breeze felt refreshing as she walked to the church, humming the melodies to her favorite hymns. She found her friends, Lucy and Vanessa huddled and talking at the bottom of the stairs at the entrance of Santa Maria.

"She did what? No way." Lucy commented on the latest gossip.

"You know Virginia, she'll sleep with anybody." confirmed Vanessa.

Sonia was in no mood to engage in the session this morning. She just waved hello and went up to the sanctuary. She sat about two pews from the altar looking at the places to her right thinking about the days when Miguel Angel and Marisol sat in this space with her. Miguel would squirm in his brown suit jacket and fidget with his tie, while Marisol hid her face behind the program, peeking out from time to time.

Sonia no longer made them get up and come with her. She wanted this decision to come from them.

As the mass continued, Sonia found more peace of mind. She listened to the scripture readings, gave the sign of peace and made sure to shake hands with people who were not close to her pew. She listened to the homily and decided she would not attend confession.

Her body moved from side to side as she swayed to the organist playing the final hymn 'Lord You Have Come to the Lakeshore.' This comforted her.

"Please join us for coffee and refreshments in the fellowship hall. The mass has ended you may go in peace." said Father Dino.

Sonia walked downstairs to the meeting hall, took her coffee and sat next to a couple and a child that she hadn't seen before. The little girl reminded her of Marisol.

"Hello. I'm Sonia. Are you new here?"

"Humberto", replied the man. "My wife, Sandra and that little one hiding behind her is our daughter Consuelo."

"Hi, Consuelo." Sonia bent over and met her at eye level. The girl shook Sonia's outstretched hand.

"Do you like chocolate cake?" asked Sonia.

Consuelo nodded yes.

Sonia walked over to a table, took a slice and gave it to the child.

"Thank you."

"You are very welcome and I hope you decide to come back." said Sonia to them as she got ready to go home.

The following day at work Sonia finished typing a memo for her supervisor, Mr. Reynolds then took the Congress Line subway home. She walked the four blocks from the Chicago Avenue station to Big Angel's garage.

The sounds of wrenches turning and the smell of oil permeated the shop. A mechanic took the time to whistle at Sonia as she walked by him.

"Excuse me sir. I am here to speak to your boss." said Sonia ignoring his ignorance.

He put down an oil can and pointed to Big Angel's office, which was up some stairs and almost in the center, allowing Big Angel to keep an eye on everyone and everything.

She walked right to his office to find Big Angel talking to two men wearing fedoras and trench coats. Sonia knocked on the open door and Big Angel looked past the two men.

"May I please speak with you sir?" asked Sonia.

"Señora Concepción. What brings you here?" replied Big Angel.

Sonia remained silent and just looked at him.

Big Angel put his arms around both men leading them to the door. "Look, fellas. Come by tonight at about nine. We'll have some high suckers ready to play. Lots of money to be made."

"Thanks. See you tonight."

"Now you have all of my attention." said Big Angel, looking at Sonia as he smiled, sat down and pointed to the chair in front of his desk.

Sonia did not want to sit down but she wasn't about to be rude. She looked at the calendar of naked women pinned to the wall behind Big Angel and sighed.

"What's the matter? You have a problem with that?" he said pointing to the calendar.

"It's your office Mr. Cintron."

"Call me Big Angel, please. What can I do for you?"

"Mr. Cintron you have been good to my son. He can fix most problems with cars and loves doing it. But..... I must say...... that I am worried. I do not want him to work for you at your new garage."

"What's wrong with my money?"

Big Angel took a sip of coffee then put the cup on his desk. He sat back in his chair with his fingers intertwined. His black hair was always combed neatly and even in this space where dirt was flying all over the place, he did not let any dust accumulate on his Florsheim shoes.

"Nothing is wrong with your money. It's just that Miguel Angel is very happy working out of Mrs. Larsen's garage at her home."

Mrs. Larsen was a widow whose husband had died in the Korean War. As a child Miguel Angel always carried her groceries home for her. She would be walking with them and when she got to the block where he was with his friends, Miguel Angel would stop playing and take her bags, that each year had become increasingly heavier for her. She never forgot that. So when Miguel Angel needed a place to work on cars she immediately offered her garage.

"Miguel Angel can make a whole lot more money running my place than just being an alley mechanic." He took another sip of coffee. "I love the taste of this coffee. It's almost a perfect cup. Where are my manners? Would you like some?"

15

"No thank you Mr. Cintron."

"Big Angel please."

"Yesterday morning we heard gun shots coming from here and we saw the ambulance take away a dead man. What you do is your business Mr. Cintron but please this life is not for my son.. a smart businessman like you can find somebody else."

"I could…. but I trust Miguel Angel."

"But… I am afraid of what can happen to him."

"Nothing is going to happen to him. I give you my word. At my new place he will just be making sure that all of the mechanics are doing their job right, and that nobody is trying to rip me off."

"Rip you off?" asked Sonia.

"Yeah, like stealing parts and selling them out in the street, stuff like that goes on all the time. But it won't happen if Miguel Angel is there keeping an eye on things for me." replied Big Angel.

"Mr. Cintron everyone knows that illegal gambling and other dangerous things happen here."

"But it was okay for him to come here when he was a kid, right? Look people talk about things without even knowing if they're true. A lot of stories Señora Concepción. Don't believe everything you hear."

"And the man who was killed here Sunday, that was no story."

"No, just a man who made a foolish choice. This is business Señora Concepción, and I am going to open another shop. Miguel Angel is a man."

"Yes, he is, but he will always be my son. I'm sure that you can find someone else to work for you."

"Señora Concepción. I'm sorry, but Miguel Angel will work for me."

Sonia knew that there was nothing left to be said. She got up, straightened her dress and walked out of his office.

After the conversation with Big Angel the days passed on and there was an underlying tension at home between Sonia and Miguel Angel. She did not want to bring up the topic of him working for Big Angel out of fear that it would turn into another argument as it did two weeks ago. Miguel Angel could not understand why she would want to deny him the opportunity to manage a shop for Big Angel.

"Mami I'm not a little kid! I know what I'm doing!" Miguel said to her, right before he slammed the door in Sonia's face.

At that moment she came to the realization that the more she tried to convince him, the more he was going to resist. This didn't stop her from thinking of possible ways to reach him. She even lit a candle and prayed to Santa Barbara asking her for divine intervention, so that her son could understand the risks that he would be taking.

CHAPTER 3

*M*arisol did not want to take either side in the situation between her brother and mother. She continued writing poetry in her journal, making floral arrangements at the greenhouse, and reading at the public library. As a child during the hot summer months she was one of those who preferred getting lost in books as opposed to splashing water and swimming at the pool.

On this spring day she was walking to the library enjoying the warmth of the sun against her skin. She loved the smell of the bacalaitos and alcapurrias as she walked past Rafael's Cafe, making a mental note to get one on her way back.

As she was approaching the building, she saw a young woman about her age standing to the side of the entrance. When Marisol looked at the red bandana wrapped around the woman's beautiful afro, she touched her own hair that felt so stretched and tight against her skin. She had seen this woman standing in front of the library many times before, passing out newspapers and engaging people in conversation. And she admired the way that she could talk to all kinds of people with poise and confidence.

"Here you go, come to the Cultural Center this Friday night, for free music and poetry," the woman told the passersby. Everyone stopped and acknowledged her, even those who ended up throwing away the flyer once they saw a garbage can. But for those who would stop and talk to this woman, she would connect with them in a deep and personal way while making the case to fight for Puerto Rican independence.

"That's why we need to be free, brother!" she told a man who had stopped to listen.

"You're crazy. We can't survive on our own," answered the man.

"Why not? That's what they want you to think that we are too small to take care of ourselves. You know us Boricuas can do anything!" The woman answered with a strong yet gentle conviction. "Look why don't you come check us out Friday night?"

"I might come for the music. This band can jam," said the man while taking the flyer.

"Then just come jam. That's good enough" replied the woman.

Uncharacteristically Marisol walked up to the woman and started talking to her.

"Can I see the paper?"

Marisol saw that the woman was a bit surprised.

"Of course you can my sister. What's your name?"

"Marisol." She took a quick glance at the headline; it read, "We Are a Colony Not a Commonwealth!"

"My name is Valentina, Valentina Sinmiedo," she said as she accepted Marisol's five dollars. On the occasion when people stopped to engage, a dollar was considered a good donation. "Thanks for giving to the cause Marisol. It seems like you know about what's going on."

"A little bit. My mom sometimes talks about Albizu Campos leading the sugar cane workers' strike and things like that."

"Wow. You're way ahead of the game."

"I wouldn't say all that."

"Hey most people don't even know who Albizu Campos is. Look we're having this really cool event Friday night at the Cultural Center. Here's the flyer. Come check us out."

Valentina looked at the journal and pen that Marisol was carrying.

"You like poetry, right? Come so you can hear some."

Marisol walked into the library and Valentina continued her work of enlightening people about the cause.

Friday night came and found Marisol watering and pruning the last plants for the day. She was not completely lost, as usual, in the rich colors of the flowers. The idea of going to the Cultural Center to hear the words of poets who were brave enough to share their words appealed to her. She did not go home for dinner that evening out of fear that if she did, she would come up with an excuse to not go. Instead, she called Sonia to let her know that she would be coming home a little later than usual.

Marisol had never been inside the Betances Cultural Center, even though just about everyone in the neighborhood knew exactly where it was. When she got there she was greeted by an older woman with a warm, welcoming smile.

"Come on in, mija. I am Elena. It's two dollars for the cause, but if you don't have it don't worry. Join us anyway."

Marisol went into her purse and took out two dollars and handed it to the woman who put it away in a cigar box.

"We also have a plate of arroz con habichuelas and chicken if you would like to eat. "This is your first time here right mija?" asked Elena.

"Yes," replied Marisol.

"Give this ticket to the man in front of the kitchen and he'll give you a plate. It's on us."

After getting her food Marisol made her way to an unoccupied table. She found the food to be delicious and the sound of bongos, guitars and cuatros combining to make folkloric music energized her in a way that was also soothing. It was interesting for her to see families consisting of young couples and their children. To one side of the stage stood the Puerto Rican flag and on the other stood a flag that she did not recognize at first, but would later come to learn that it was the flag of Lares, Puerto Rico.

After a while the music was tuned off and a man walked past the people and on to the center of the stage.

"Good evening my brothers and sisters. We welcome you here and it's unbelievable to think that you are still alive. When you came through that door we didn't knock you out and then put you in a big pot and boil you until you were ready to eat! See independendistas are not blood thirsty cannibals ready to eat your babies."

The audience laughed. He had the ability to make light of the sad fact that often people are taught to fear the very ones who are fighting for their freedom.

"My name is Juan Sanchez and I am a member of the event planning team here at Betances," continued the man.

"Tonight we have 3 poets from right here in the heart of our barrio and a tremendous band that is going to have you dancing, 'Sol y Luna.' Please remember that any donation that you can give is for supporting our after school center and youth outreach program. Please give as generously as you can. Now let's hear it for the first poet who will delight us with her magic lines, Lola Bermudez."

A diminutive woman came onto the stage and thanked everyone in a barely audible whisper. But when she started reciting her poetry her voice boomed with a presence that drew everyone right to the center of the stage as if she were a magnet.

Three more poets shared their words, then it came time for the band to start playing. Two young men came out and created a small space for dancing by moving a few tables to the back of the room.

Juan Sanchez came back out and introduced the musical group, Sol y Luna.

It was a small group of six and they created a festive atmosphere from the moment they hit the first note. Marisol was surprised to see a man standing in front of her with his hand in position to take hers, asking her to dance.

"Oh no." Marisol shook her head frightened by the possibility of people watching her dance. The only time that she ever dared dance was when she was sweeping or mopping the floor at home. As soon as she heard a song that she loved on the radio she would turn up the volume and dance with incredible energy. She wouldn't even think about dancing in front of people, not even at family parties.

"Look it's easy," said the gentleman as he took a couple of steps in front of her in perfect rhythm with the congas. It was right at that point that Valentina appeared in front of him and took his hand. Marisol smiled and delighted in watching the dancers move and turn in sync with each other. The song ended and Valentina came back to the table where Marisol was sitting.

"You made it! I'm so happy that you decided to come!" said Valentina as if Marisol was the only person who she had told about the event. "Did you dig the poetry?"

"It was beautiful," answered Marisol.

"Did Lola make you cry?"

"Almost."

"Sorry that I got here a little late, but I had to help my brother. He was feeling a little sick," said Valentina.

"I hope he gets better."

"Yeah you and me both." Valentina said, then took a sip of wine and inhaled the sweet scent of freedom that these events produced, and sat back in her chair.

The band continued their set as people joyfully danced. One couple was dancing with their two small children in between them, making Marisol think about her mother and father displaying affection towards each other.

Suddenly the band leader raised his hand, cueing the band to stop. He slowly counted them in for a new song. The piano player came in first and the rest of them followed. It was a familiar up - tempo song by Ismael Rivera, played in the form of a ballad. This caught the attention of the audience. They stopped talking with each other and just listened. In the middle of the piece the saxophone player got into a beautiful haunting solo. It was as if the instrument was longing for a love that it has never felt. The song finished with some soft notes on the piano and the people clapped out of deep appreciation for being part of a wonderful moment.

"That was Omar Burgos on the sax" said the bass player who was also the leader.

"Ooohhh he can play my instrument anytime," whispered Valentina in Marisol's ear.

Marisol blushed as she put her hand to her mouth and looked down at the floor.

"You're bold," said Marisol.

"No, I just express how I'm feeling. Men can talk about sex all day long, brag about their million conquests, and all the women that they're going to have. So what's wrong with me telling you that a guy is hot and I would like to give him some of my good lovin'?"

Marisol erupted into a loud laugh, and let her body move with it.

"Thanks for telling me about tonight, Valentina. I'm going home."

Valentina looked at her watch. "It's only 11. Do you want to do something?"

"No. My mom is probably still up and worried."

"You're what 20?" asked Valentina.

"19 actually"

"That's alright. I'm sure that she loves you and is just looking out for you."

They stood up and Valentina gave her a big hug and thanked her for coming to the Cultural Center.

"Hey do you want to get together at Raul's Cafe or some other place one day Marisol?"

"Yes."

They exchanged phone numbers and Marisol left while Valentina started going around the room talking and laughing with people.

When Marisol got home she found Sonia in her pajamas and nightgown asleep, sitting on the living room sofa. She walked up to her mother and kissed her on her forehead.

"Bendición Mami."

"Oh, mija. What time is it? asked Sonia.

"It's about midnight."

"Where were you?"

"They had a beautiful night of poetry and music at the Betances Cultural Center."

"Those crazy people?"

"Mami you know they're not crazy."

"If you say so. Come here, let me talk to you."

Sonia gestured for Marisol to sit down next to her.

"I'm really worried about your brother."

"Why?"

Sonia stood up and gave Marisol an incredulous look.

"You know why. That thug, Big Angel is going to open another shop and Miguel Angel, your....... brother is going to help him run it!'

"But m-"

"But nothing. Don't you care about your brother?"

Marisol looked on the living room table and saw two bottles of beer. Sonia rarely drank alone.

"Mami you know how Migue is, if he wants to work for Big Angel he's going to do it."

"Talk to him, please. Explain to him how dangerous it could be. He won't listen to me."

"So what makes you think he'll listen to me?"

"It's just that, just that, your father"

25

Sonia sat back down and started crying.

"I don't want him to end up like your father."

Marisol walked over to Sonia and held her, and tried to reassure her that Miguel Angel had common sense and that he would be able to navigate the treacherous waters of working for a man like Big Angel.

Sonia fell asleep and Marisol went to her mother's bedroom, got a blanket, and laid it over her.

"Good night mami." She kissed Sonia on the forehead again and went to her bedroom.

reakfast the following Monday was particularly quiet. Even if they all had to get to work and there was little time, Sonia always managed to find out about how her children were really doing.

Miguel Angel finished eating his fried eggs and sopped up the last bit of yolk that was left on his plate with a piece of his Kaiser roll. He sat in front of Sonia and held the roll in his hand, looking past her.

"What's wrong son?"

"Nothing"

"Really? Come on I know you."

"You talked with Big Angel."

Miguel Angel did not want to disrespect his mother but he couldn't understand why she was trying to take away the chance for him to feel alive, work with his hands and immediately fix engine problems that for other mechanics would take a few days just to figure out was wrong. He thought that she must know how working for Big Angel would increase his status, and he would gain even more respect. Why couldn't she understand that he knew how to handle himself and would just ignore all of the other things that went on at the garage? Big Angel would make sure that he didn't get into any kind of trouble and protect him. He knew this for a fact.

Miguel Angel started thinking about an incident that had happened when he was twelve years old. He was coming back from the park on his way to Big Angel's garage. When he got there, he was still wearing his baseball cap and glove while holding a ball in his hand and looking down at the ground. Big Angel saw him and called him over.

"Hey Migue! Come here kid!" He tapped him lightly on the head. "We're going to the Sox game tonight to see Dick Allen crush some balls out of the park. Wanna come?"

Miguel Angel half - heartedly looked at him and said, "Yeah."

"You were over at the park playing ball today right? What's the matter did you strike out all day?" asked Big Angel, laughing.

"No. A man was there."

"At the park Migue?"

Big Angel stopped laughing and bent over to be at eye level with Miguel Angel and put his strong heavy hand on his shoulder.

"Did anything happen with this man?" asked Big Angel.

"He said weird stuff."

"What weird stuff?"

"Like opening my pants, his mouth"

The expression on Big Angel's face became eerily calm as he was able to reassure Miguel Angel that he had done nothing wrong, while holding down the anger that was rising in him like a high tide about to crash into the shore.

"Is that right? What did he look like Migue?"

"Black hair and a beard"

Big Angel looked up at his office and found Oscar. Oscar was six feet four and weighed about 250 pounds. He had played football in high school and rarely talked to anyone.

"Oscar! Oscar come down here!" Big Angel called loudly over the sound of the drills, hammers and engines.

Oscar made his way down to Big Angel.

"I want you to go back to the park with Migue here. The kid is going to show you a man. You'll know him when you see him right Migue?"

Miguel Angel looked up at Oscar and Big Angel and noticed how Oscar listened to him, nodding to confirm that he understood Big Angel.

"When you see that man, I want you to take care of him. Got it?"

"All the way, Big Angel?" asked Oscar.

"No, just enough to let him know that a grown man has no business talking to a little boy about his pants. Know what I mean?"

"Now go ahead Migue go back with Oscar and play catch."

A few hours later, the police found a man in a gangway of a building across the street from the park. His face was a bloody mess and both legs were broken.

Miguel Angel never saw the man come around the park again.

Sonia did not find out about this incident. If she had, she would have understood why Miguel Angel felt safe being in the presence of Big Angel and why working for him now at the age of 20 did not feel risky at all.

"Mami don't talk to Big Angel about me"

"Why not?"

"It's embarrassing. I have to go, bendición."

"Dios te bendiga, mijo."

After asking for his mother's blessing Miguel Angel was off to Mrs. Larsen's to spend his day using his mind and hands underneath the hood of cars.

Later that week Sonia tried her best to not let herself be distracted at work.

"Sonia why am I holding this message in my hand?" Mr. Reynolds asked Sonia. He had walked from his office to Sonia's desk in the reception area delicately holding the piece of paper from the message pad.

"It's for you from the furnace company, Mr. Reynolds," answered Sonia.

"How long have you been here now, Sonia?"

"About five years"

"Who handles these matters, dear?" Mr. Reynolds continued towering over Sonia's desk.

"Mr. Thompson" Sonia answered while taking the message from Mr. Reynolds. She apologized to him and realized that it was his way of checking in on her. He had always been kind from the time that she started working there. He took pleasure in looking at Miguel Angel's and Marisol's school pictures every year, and made sure to ask Sonia about Miguel's diving meets and Marisol's love for reading. In turn Mr. Reynolds shared stories about his trips to London with her. He was a closeted gay man who was able to experience life to the fullest out in the open in a place that offered him some amount of anonymity. That's why whenever he was going on a vacation there, Sonia could tell by his big smile and much improved disposition.

"Sonia …. the other morning I found several errors in your tuition payments report. Is there something going on?" asked Mr. Reynolds.

"No, I'm fine."

He just stood there with his hands on his hips and his head bent a bit to the side.

"Why don't you come to my office for a second dear."

Sonia got up and walked with him to his office. The other secretary looked down at her desk, sensing that Sonia was going to be reprimanded for the tuition report, giving phone messages to the wrong people and several other mistakes that were very uncharacteristic of her.

Mr. Reynolds sat down behind his desk unbuttoned his suit coat, making himself more comfortable.

"I am sorry about the messages and report, Mr. Reynolds."

"Don't worry about that Sonia. Now tell me what is really on your mind."

Sonia started crying and Mr. Reynolds gently pushed a box of Kleenex to her side of the desk.

"It is my son. He has decided to work for a very dangerous man."

"I see Sonia. How old is Miguel Angel now?"

"Twenty"

"Unfortunately, my dear there is probably nothing that you can do. You probably can't or don't want to go to the police because that would just make matters worse. Am I right?"

"Yes," said Sonia, as she dried the last tear from her eyes and composed herself, taking a deep breath. Mr. Reynolds saying this had some what of a calming effect on her as she began thinking about other ways to handle this situation.

Mr. Reynolds leaned forward and looked directly into Sonia's eyes.

"You know that I am very fond of you, and the mistakes you've made recently are no big deal to me, things happen, but Mr. Thompson and Mr. Settler are not exactly the forgiving kind."

"Thank you Mr. Reynolds." She looked at the picture of him smiling in front of Big Ben and asked him when he was taking his next trip. He said that he was leaving in two weeks and she sensed that this was part of the reason why she was sitting in his office. She knew that he was well intentioned in his advice to her, but this also gave him an opportunity to talk about why he was really going to London. He was looking forward to spending time with Michael, his lover. She was the only person at work with whom he could share this.

"I appreciate you looking out for me Mr. Reynolds. Thank you." She stood up and opened the door and got ready to walk back to her desk, then turned around when Mr. Reynolds called her name.

"Sonia…. thank you."

CHAPTER 5

*M*iguel Angel had just arrived at Mrs. Larsen's and opened the garage door. His friend Luis had a cousin by the name of Omar. He was a musician visiting from New York, to help Luis record his first album. They had arranged to meet there by 9. On time, Omar drove up in his black '79 Chevrolet Nova.

Omar rolled down the window and lowered his sun glasses.

"Hey. What's up? Miguel Angel?"

"Yeah. Just drive it in here." Miguel Angel pointed to the right side of the garage. He looked at Omar's immaculately shined leather shoes, and neatly ironed pleated black dress pants and wondered why he was dressed so sharply just to bring his car in for a repair.

"Cool." Omar parked the car and then came out to talk with Miguel Angel.

"Omar, Omar Burgos, man." Omar extended his arm and they shook hands.

"My cousin Luis said that you're a good mechanic."

Miguel Angel nodded yes and asked, "What's wrong with it?"

"The oil light keeps coming on but I just had it changed two weeks ago."

"Pop the hood."

Miguel Angel went underneath it and began working in his usual swift yet meticulous manner. Omar walked out of the garage and started observing the neighborhood. He waved to two older women who had just appeared on their porch in their bathrobes.

"Hey man do…. people…. always come out of their houses dressed like that?"

Miguel Angel already had a good idea who Omar was talking about but peaked from underneath the hood to see in which direction Omar was looking.

"Two old ladies?" asked Miguel Angel.

"Yeah, in their bathrobes, just out there on their porch looking down on the street," answered Omar.

"They don't bother"

"Too bad they aren't a couple of fine ladies. Speaking of that, where do all the beautiful women hang out around here? I was playing music the other night at some cultural center and it was just alright. Know what I mean?"

"Sensor's good. The oil might not be going anywhere."

"Cool. Can you fix that?"

"Yeah"

"How long is it going to take?" asked Omar.

"We gotta get the parts first."

"No problem. Where do we get them?"

Miguel Angel pointed in the direction of Steve's Auto Parts and they started walking. Once they got there, Miguel Angel ordered the pump then quickly gathered all of the parts needed for the repair.

"How did you learn about cars man?" asked Omar.

"Started at Big Angel's"

"What's that?"

"A garage. They taught me."

"I see"

They walked up to the register.

Miguel Angel noticed how the cashier, Sylvia, was smiling and in one second she looked Omar up and down and took in every single detail.

"Hi Migue. Who's your friend?" asked Sylvia.

"I'm just fixing his car." Miguel Angel responded, thinking to himself that she rarely had anything to say. She always rang up customers and then took care of the next person in line.

"$35 Migue," said Sylvia.

"Here you go lovely lady. Sylvia, that's a beautiful name" said Omar as he handed her two twenty dollar bills, looking at her name stitched into her jacket.

"And since a gentleman never asks a lady for her number right away, let me give you my card. I'll be playing a solo set at, The Shore, tonight."

The man standing behind them who was waiting in line to buy windshield wipers loudly cleared his throat.

Sylvia rolled her eyes at the customer, took the card read it and asked, "Oooh a musician, what do you play?"

Omar leaned forward slightly, enough to show interest but not giving the impression of being desperate. "A little bit of everything baby, but tonight it'll be just me, my guitar and my songs. I come on at 7."

They paid for the oil pump and started walking back to Mrs. Larsen's garage. "Sylvia likes you."

"Who?" Omar said to Miguel Angel.

"At the auto parts, just now," said Miguel Angel almost in disbelief.

"Yeah, yeah she's alright."

"Women like musicians?" asked Miguel Angel.

"Like? No, they love....... musicians. See man, most daughters from the time that they're little girls, all they hear from their mothers is to stay away from us, because we're players and break women's hearts. Then, when that little girl turns into a woman, she wants that forbidden fruit. But you still have to play it right and be smooth. As a matter of fact the rap, that gift of gab, is even more important than playing music, if you want to get in with the ladies."

Miguel Angel finished replacing the oil pump without any wasted movement or action.

"Hey I've seen cats work on cars before but you're like a surgeon man. You should call yourself Dr. Miguel."

"Thanks, man."

"I'm surprised that this car made it all the way from New York. I'll probably be coming to you for some more repairs."

"No problem."

"Say I saw that Mickey's Burgers place up the street on the way here. Is it any good?"

"Good burgers man"

"Want to come with me? My treat."

"I have to go home and wash up first."

"Thats cool. Let's go, get in."

Miguel Angel got in the car and they drove to his home.

"I'll wait for you here," said Omar.

Sitting in his car listening to Jose Feliciano singing 'Light my Fire' Omar didn't even notice Marisol walking past him, on her way home. Marisol remembered Omar from the night at the Cultural Center and wondered why he was parked in front of their home, looking like he was waiting for someone.

"Hey Migue. There's this guy in a car right in front, you know him?"

"Black car?"

"Yes"

"He's Luis' cousin."

"I saw him playing music the other night."

"I changed his oil pump. We're going to Mickey's now."

"He can really play the sax you know."

"Do girls like that?" asked Miguel thinking about Sylvia's reaction to meeting Omar.

"Are you thinking about taking out that old guitar that papi gave you for Christmas when you were seven?"

Miguel Angel blushed and said, "Maybe"

Marisol went to her room and got her journal before heading back out to the greenhouse.

"See you tonight Migue."

"See you."

Sonia woke up Sunday morning to hear the sound of notes plucked clumsily on a guitar. She walked to Miguel Angel's room and found him sitting on the edge of his bed in his pajamas, playing.

"That's the one your father gave you when you were seven," said Sonia.

"Yeah"

"It's so old."

"My friend put new strings on it."

"Well, I'll let you keep playing." She walked away, smiling, remembering how Rafael had worked two double shifts a week for a month so that they could afford to buy presents for Marisol and Miguel Angel. On Christmas Eve, after getting off work and taking two buses in below zero weather and walking in snow that came up over his ankles, Rafael made it home. He warmed up with coffee, walked to their bedroom closet, took out the hidden guitar and gave it to Miguel Angel.

For Sonia, this was a beautiful memory, and it made her think about Miguel Angel having lost his innocence to the point where he would even consider working for a man like Big Angel.

She received another pleasant surprise when Marisol came out of her room dressed and ready to go to church with her. Marisol did not have her hair in a tight bun, as she usually did. Her reddish-brown curls flowed freely form her the top of her head to just above her shoulders, and small gold looped earrings accentuated her beauty. Sonia stood in front of her not knowing what to say.

"Come on mami. We don't want to be late."

"You're going with me today?"

"I want to hear this new priest, Father Alberto."

"That's right. Father Gus is retiring. How do you know this?" Sonia did not want to spoil the way the day had started but was curious. After all, Marisol hadn't been to a Mass with her in quite some time.

"Valentina told me."

"Who?"

"She's the one who invited me to hear poetry and music at Betances the other night. You'll see her."

Sonia couldn't understand why the atheists at the Betances Cultural Center would be so interested in the new priest, but she decided that her happiness for Marisol's new found motivation for attending church with her was more important. Once they were there and Father Alberto started his homily, Sonia easily made the connection between Father Alberto and the Betances Cultural Center.

"The young man walked away from Jesus crying because he did not want to give up his riches. No. He could not live in a world order that intentionally, listen carefully, I said intentionally creates masses of people living in poverty, so that a privileged few can live in luxury. And is that not what we see today? If we are blessed by God, then we must stand up against injustice and poverty! That is what Jesus calls us to do." Father Alberto, a tall man with high cheekbones, brown eyes and bronze skin, said these words with an intense passion that demonstrated the depths of his commitment. By design he had been transferred to this parish in Chicago all the way from El Salvador. It didn't take him long to connect with like minded people, the members of the Betances Cultural Center. That definitely was not the outcome that the church wanted.

The Mass concluded with some feeling overjoyed over finally hearing a priest at this parish talk about the revolutionary power of the gospel. While others were upset over hearing words that verged on being blasphemous.

Sonia and Marisol walked down the front stairs of the church. Marisol heard the voice of a young woman coming through loud and clear amidst all of the people, who laughed, talked and caught up on the events of their week. Sonia turned and saw Valentina coming dressed in red with a white bandana tied around her perfectly round afro.

"Valentina! I love your colors." said Marisol as she hugged Valentina, then turned to Sonia.

"Mami this is Valentina."

"Mucho gusto Señora Concepción."

"Un placer nena. So did you come for Jesus or Chango? asked Sonia.

Valentina smiled and said, "You know our culture."

Sonia knew that the colors of the Yoruba deity Chango were red and white. As a child when she was sick in bed with a bad stomach ache, her mother would kneel at her side with a rosary in her hand, as she invoked the name of the Orishas while rubbing hot oil on Sonia's stomach to ease the pain. Sonia had continued this tradition with her children. This comforting ritual combined the Yoruba religion with a Christianity that had been imposed on African slaves by the Spaniards.

"How did you two meet again?" asked Sonia.

"In front of the library. She's the one who invited me to the cultural center." answered Marisol.

"Yes, yes the Betances Center," said Sonia with an expression that gave away her ideas about the people who work at the center being crazy activists who were out of touch with reality.

"Señora Concepción, you should come visit us sometime," said Valentina.

Sonia was about to answer, but then Valentina saw Father Alberto walking towards them.

"Alberto!" Valentina hugged Father Alberto and some of the parishioners who heard were caught a little off guard that she didn't use the word "Father." Some of the women poked at each other with their elbows while pointing at Valentina and the newly arrived priest hugging.

"You're coming tomorrow to work with the after school kids, right?" asked Valentina as she turned Father Alberto towards Sonia and Marisol to introduce them.

"Alberto, this is my friend Marisol and her mother, Sonia."

"Pleasure to meet you." Father Alberto shook their hands and Sonia felt the calluses on his palms that came from working the land. He was not only preaching about being in solidarity with small family farmers in El Salvador, he worked side by side with them sowing corn in the fields.

Upon feeling his hands, it was clear to Sonia that his delivery and interpretation of the gospel was not only talk.

"Father Alberto. Welcome to our church" said Sonia. "You're spending time at the Betances Cultural Center?"

"I tutor the kids in the after school program." answered Father Alberto.

"That is very different from the work you did in El Salvador no?"

"In some ways yes. I love it. At school many of these kids are told that they're failures and won't amount to anything, but at Betances they are loved and given opportunities to learn."

Sonia and Marisol immediately thought of Miguel Angel and Father Alberto's words resonated with them.

Feeling all of this positive energy Valentina smiled from ear to ear. As a friend she was happy to be connecting with Marisol's mother and as an activist she was thrilled to see Father Albert engaging with the community.

"Hey, Sra. Concepción, Marisol and I are going for a bite to eat at Raul's Cafe. Come with us," said Valentina.

"I would love to, their food is delicious but thank you, I'm going over to talk with Lucy and some of my other friends." Sonia felt so happy that Marisol was coming out of her shell and yet she was a bit worried that this new found freedom was coming from the ideas and experience that Marisol was having from spending time at the Betances Cultural Center.

"You two go and enjoy." With that Sonia said goodbye to the three of them and made her way to Lucy.

"Hay Dios mio. I couldn't believe what he was saying. And did you see him kiss those girls?" Lucy was getting into the gossip and soon to be fast spreading rumors about newly arrived Father Alberto.

"You don't know anything about him Lucy" Sonia interjected.

Lucy still wore a bee hive hairdo and took advantage of Sonia getting into the conversation by taking a few more puffs of her menthol cigarette. Her husband Francisco Figueroa, also known as "Fast Frankie," stood next to her. In the company of her friends, when no one else was around, Lucy always bragged about his sexual prowess. According to Lucy his penis could penetrate to depths unknown in any woman, and toe curling loud orgasmic sex was just about an everyday experience.

"Sonia. You're coming Friday right?" asked Lucy.

"Friday?"

"You forgot already? My party. I'm visiting my mother in Connecticut for a month. Frankie is going to make sure we have some fun before I go."

"Yeah, Sonia. You should come." Frankie had been silent the whole time but Sonia noticed how he made sure to express his desire for having her at the party. Sonia felt both uncomfortable and strangely flattered by the way Frankie looked at her. It had been some time since Sonia had felt consistent companionship from a man. For the sake of her children, she suppressed her sexuality.

Sonia waved good bye to her friends and started walking home. It was getting warmer and she could hear the sounds of salsa music coming from cars passing by with their windows rolled down. She felt the sun a little hotter now that it was afternoon, and she took off her jacket. On the walk home, her conversation with Mr. Reynolds came to mind. At that moment it hit her that she would have to take matters into her own hands. She was determined to make sure that Miguel Angel did not get in too deep with Big Angel.

CHAPTER 6

*R*aul's Cafe had pictures of musicians performing in concerts and street festivals on the walls. Raul also had framed photos of children playing in open fire hydrants and of people walking proudly in the Puerto Rican parade. Music came from the jukebox as people smiled and sang along to their favorite songs in between bites.

"This is beautiful writing Mari. Look at you, I love your hair and earrings. I can tell that you're loving the Julia De Burgos book," said Valentina as she handed Marisol her journal. Marisol had not shared it with anybody and although she had not known her for long, she had confidence that Valentina would not ridicule or put down her writing or for that matter anything else about her.

"What's your favorite Julia piece so far?," asked Valentina.

"Yo Misma Fui Mi Ruta"

"Dig. Love that piece! I can find my own way without a man telling me how to get there," declared Valentina.

"How did you become so involved in this whole independence thing?" Marisol asked.

"I was kind of born into it. My uncle was killed in the Ponce Massacre. I remember how papi would come to tears whenever he talked about his little brother Ismael going off to a march on Palm Sunday in his clean, pressed shirt. My father said that Ismael had been talking about it the entire week, and when the day came, he hadn't slept at all the night before. 'Til this day pops says that he can still hear the sounds of my grandmother screaming when she was told that her son was one of the nineteen who were killed when they were led to a place from which there was no way to get out and then bullets came flying from every direction. Why? They didn't have to die like that."

Marisol noticed the change in Valentina's voice as she talked about this. Then she saw a slight frown and Valentina's jaw tightened and her eyebrows came closer together.

"But the real reason, Mari is because, if I wasn't in the movement, I wouldn't be alive." Valentina put down her fork and folded her hands almost wringing them with a very slight tremble.

"My brother Gamaliel was the most fun-loving guy that you'd ever meet. At parties people always gathered around him to hear and laugh at his stories. I even remember one time we were driving in the pouring rain, and he saw a couple stranded on the side of Lake Shore Drive. He got off at the next exit, then got back on in the opposite direction. He went and changed their tire. He saw people who needed help, and he did, no questions asked. They turned out to be a rich doctor and his wife who were staying at some fancy hotel downtown for a conference. They offered him money, but Gamaliel didn't take it. All of this changed when he came back from Vietnam." Valentina didn't say anything for a minute or so, then she began to cry. Marisol reassured her by placing her hand on hers.

"What happened to him over there?" asked Marisol. She remembered that as a little girl she had overheard a conversation between Sonia and her friends. They drank coffee in the kitchen and talked about their sons and brothers coming back from

Vietnam and not being able to hold a job, suffered nervous breakdowns, became alcoholics, addicts or both. In between these stories they also laughed and told jokes to try and ease the pain.

"He......, when..." continued Valentina. "When he came back after a year there, he barely said anything. He would smile from time to time, but no more funny stories or anything like that. Sometimes in the middle of the night he'd wake up screaming."Stop, stop they're babies, God damn it, stop!" "The smell of burning flesh of women and families running from their huts stayed in his mind. He couldn't get rid of it."

"Valentina, it's okay if you don't want to keep talking about this."

"No, Mari. I still haven't answered your question. See, the worst thing that he brought back with him was the need to shoot that junk into his veins every single day, all day if he could. He had the music blasting one day in his room, and I was studying for a chemistry test. I knocked on his door to tell him to turn it down, and walked in to find him with a belt wrapped tight around his left arm, his head dangling, and his right hand holding a syringe. Deep down it was no surprise because he had been showing us all of the signs, we just chose to ignore them."

"What did your family do when they found out about it?" asked Marisol.

"My parents are real old-fashioned Puerto Rican, and you know they didn't go for that drug stuff. My mother would freak out if she knew I smoke weed."

"You do?" asked Marisol with a curiosity that implied she was interested in trying it.

"We can check some out later" said Valentina as she smiled, laughed lightly, and continued the story.

"How is your brother doing today?" asked Marisol.

"He isn't. He's buried at St. Boniface Cemetery. The dope, the nightmares, the stealing from everyone to support his habit drove him even crazier than he already was. One day he tried robbing a liquor store with a cap gun, and the owner blew a hole through his chest. He died instantly."

Valentina slowly started rocking back and forth in her chair with her arms crossed. She just looked in front of her with a blank stare. It was as if she had cried her last tear and her well had gone completely dry.

"Valentina?"

"I can't talk about Gamaliel anymore today."

"I understand."

They finished their red beans and rice with stewed chicken, then shared a slice of flan for dessert. Valentina reminded Marisol about the Poetry Nights at the Cultural Center, but Marisol wasn't quite ready for that. She was slowly becoming a different woman, having been moved by the experience of the first night at the Cultural Center, and she certainly hadn't forgotten Omar's sensuous saxophone solo. Still, the emotional scars suffered as a little girl, that came from being called a skinny broom wearing a skirt, and being ridiculed for having rough red bad hair, had not healed completely. Yet deep down she knew that she was awakening and it was only a matter of time until the night came when she would be ready to read her poems in front of an audience.

Sonia watched two couples swaying their hips to the sounds of a Tito Rodriguez mambo coming from the record player. Right in the middle of the song, the needle got stuck, and the same notes, and syllables of lyrics kept repeating and repeating.

"Hey, Frankie. It's time for a new needle man," came from one of the dancers.

That didn't matter. Somebody picked up the arm of the player and put it on the next song. They were not about to be deterred. Tonight was a chance to get away from thoughts of police brutality, signs in windows saying, "We don't rent to Puerto Ricans" and freezing apartments in the winter. It was time to celebrate. The roast pork was hot and tender. The beer was ice cold, and the whiskey went down nice and easy. It was time to party. There would be plenty of time for repentance and confession at Mass tomorrow.

Sonia wore her blue bell bottom paint suit and comfortable black two inch heels that allowed her to dance if she so happened to feel the urge.

"Sonia. Come. Eat." Lucy took Sonia by the arm and led her to the kitchen.

"Grab a plate. There's lechon, arroz con gandules, tostones, and yautia, etc.," said Lucy as she pointed to all of the delicious food. Sonia helped herself and also took a beer from the refrigerator.

"Sonia, que te pasa? Do you miss Mr. Morgan?" They both had a good laugh. Lucy and Sonia had worked together at an electric parts factory and Mr. Morgan was their overbearing boss. Sonia felt even more relaxed now that she was laughing with Lucy.

"That's right, Sonia. With everything you learned in your father's store in Puerto Rico you didn't need to take crap from Mr. Morgan! Right?" Lucy said with her arm around Sonia and holding a beer in the other.

"I didn't count the beans, weigh the rice and keep track of all the beer that papi sold for nothing," replied Sonia as she talked about the days she spent working with her father. When she was a young girl there were a few occasions in which she felt envious of her friends who were out playing in the sunshine, but for the most part she loved the responsibility that was rarely given to an adolescent girl in 1930s Puerto Rico. And when people came into settle accounts, she always marveled at her father's ability, to make calculations quickly in his mind. He was kind and loving to her and did not let a day go by without reminding her of how special she was. This treatment helped to ease the pain of her knowing from a very early age that he was a womanizer and had affairs with women that in some cases were condoned or at the minimum accepted by her mother.

Sonia looked at a man who was off to himself sitting at the end of the sofa. He was holding his face in his hands and crying.

"What's wrong with him?" asked Sonia, as she nudged Lucy.

"Ramon? Nothing. At every party he gets drunk and starts crying about how much he loves his family, but he never brings his wife."

Their attention turned to Lucy's husband who was dancing gracefully with Olga a woman who had a reputation for being loose, loving and free. Frankie gracefully led Olga to the rhythm of the music, turning with their steps perfectly in sync. With a firm yet soft hand on his partner's hips providing guidance, he had the ability to make any dancer look good. All they had to do was follow Fast Frankie.

"Sonia. Do me a favor and keep an eye on him while I'm away."

"I will," said Sonia, admiring the smooth strength in Frankie's dancing.

The party started winding down, and Sonia was helping Lucy gather and wash the dishes while the few remaining guests finished their drinks. Lucy offered those who were still there some coffee to wake up for the walk or drive home.

"Hey Sonia. I can drive you home," offered Frankie, as he walked toward Sonia.

"This Frankie of mine is always the gentleman right Sonia?" said Lucy as she pulled Frankie back towards her by the back of his untucked pinstriped shirt.

"Thanks. I already called a cab," said Sonia.

Sonia hugged Lucy goodbye and thanked her for the food, music, and most of all the laughter.

The days were getting longer and people started enjoying the warm sunshine on their skin, for they knew that this pleasure would not be possible in about four months. Omar and Miguel Angel were sitting on a park bench looking at kids playing a pick up game of basketball and hearing the clanging sound of the ball hitting off of the metal backboard. They slapped each other five and got a kick out of a kid who made a basket doing his best Dr. J impersonation. "Way to go little man!" cheered Miguel Angel.

"Can you play ball?" Miguel Angel asked Omar.

"No way, man. My pop had me practicing sax and guitar after school. No time for ball."

"Too bad."

"Kind of. Sometimes the other kids made fun of me and hated it when I was picked to be on their teams in gym class, but I love playing music you know?" explained Omar.

A ball from the baseball diamond came rolling towards their bench and they saw a girl running towards it as fast as she could pumping her arms with a baseball glove on her right hand. She picked up the ball and threw it accurately right to second base on one hop. "Way to go Jenny!" exclaimed her coach.

"Look at that girl, playing with the boys," said Omar.

"Yeah she's good," said Miguel Angel.

Omar hopped up stretched and dusted off his black dress pants. Even when he was in the park he dressed as if he was playing on stage.

"How is the guitar playing coming? Did you learn those three chords yet man?" asked Omar.

"A little bit."

"Keep playing, man. I'll show you some more. Say, is your mom still on you about going to work for that cat, what's his name?"

"Big Angel"

"Yeah"

"She thinks I'm still a kid."

"And she always will, brother. She's just looking out for you."

"I know." Miguel Angel was sitting on the bench smiling with his arms stretched out on the backrest, as he watched the games, but then he crossed them and the smile came off of his face.

"I know what I'm doing," said Miguel Angel. He expressed a fierce desire to be able to control his destiny, just like he did on the diving board as a child or under the hood of a car now as a young man.

"I hear you, man." Omar decided not to press the issue. Since arriving from New York he had not met anyone with the sincerity of Miguel Angel. Being in the music business he was around so many people who were either out for money or to exploit his talent.

"Gotta go man," said Miguel Angel as he got got up and started walking back to Mrs. Larsen's garage.

"That's right. You have to work on that guy's station wagon. Hey, we're still going to that club on Friday night, right?"

"Yeah. The Galaxy."

"I'll pick you up at 9. Unless I get a last minute gig. Sometimes they call my cousin when they need a replacement band. If that happens, I'll just meet you there."

"Cool."

"See you Migue."

Omar started walking back to his apartment. As he was leaving the park he saw two women chatting while pushing their toddlers on the swings. The children's laughter became louder the higher they went, and the women encouraged their playful display of emotion, with big bright smiles of their own. One of the women saw Omar out of the corner of her eye and turned her body to face him directly. They smiled at each other but did not exchange any words. Omar sensed an opportunity to start a conversation but he had dedicated only so much time to relaxing in the park. His music was waiting for him. When he crossed the street he looked through the windows of the library and there was Marisol with her reddish-brown flowing curls coming down the side of her face and loosely tied in a ponytail. She was wearing jeans that perfectly accentuated her lovely body. Marisol was becoming increasingly more comfortable in her skin, as the woman that she was starting to let the world see. And as beautiful as she was looking on this day, what truly attracted Omar was the look in her eyes as she selected books from the shelves. He looked at his watch, although he knew that regardless of the time he was going to go in and introduce himself.

Marisol saw Omar walking towards her and instantly recognized him. He tried playing it cool and stopped a few feet from her in the same section. Then he slowly made his way to the place where she was standing.

"You must really love reading about trees," said Omar gesturing to the book that she was holding in her hand.

Marisol looked up, turned her back to him, and walked back to her table. On it several books were spread out with a pad and pen in the middle. She took hold of the pen and continued taking notes. Omar just stood near the book shelves with nothing to say. He then walked to the table and said, "Sorry, I didn't mean to disrespect you, just trying to be friendly."

"Shush," said the librarian as she put her finger up to her lips.

Omar bowed apologizing. He had learned from his father the importance of always being a gentleman. He turned his attention back to Marisol and noticed that amongst all the books there was one about the Puerto Rican composer Rafael Hernandez. He also started to sweat just a little bit, as the library did not have any air conditioning.

"Interesting combination of books you have there," whispered Omar. "Mind if I sit and take a look at this Rafael Hernandez biography?"

"You can look at it standing up," answered Marisol.

"Thank you. My mom taught me his songs on guitar when I was a kid. Maybe I can play one for you some day?"

Marisol saw the little bead of sweat coming down the side of his forehead.

"I know you're a musician. I heard you play the other night at the Cultural Center."

"Why didn't you say so? You're over here making me sweat."

"I'm not making you do anything," said Marisol as she looked at Omar, and then continued working on her poem.

"I should be at home practicing, instead of being here admiring your beauty."

"Don't let me keep you from your music."

"Maybe I'll catch you here some other time?" said Omar, instantly regretting that he said this in the form of a weak question.

"Maybe"

Omar put the book back on the table and left. He waved at Marisol from outside and she nodded and smiled.

CHAPTER 7

*S*onia was pacing in front of the water cooler. She stopped and poured herself a cup, the sound of the bubbles rising as the water came out was loud in the empty office space. With the exception of Dolores, the cleaning lady, Sonia was the only one left. She could hear Dolores vacuuming the carpet in Mr. Reynold's office. She had waited until 6 to leave because she was meeting Francisco Figueroa at the Victory Hotel. She hadn't even gone through with the meeting yet, but was already feeling guilt and remorse for agreeing to meet the husband of a dear friend alone in a hotel, in which people met for affairs and prostitutes turned tricks.

Her mind went back to a week ago when she had made the arrangement with Francisco. She remembered knocking on their door feigning that she had forgotten that Lucy was out of town.

"Coming, coming. Who is it?" asked Francisco from inside.

"Sonia."·

With lightning speed, he removed the security chain and opened the door. He stood there with a big smile, his shirt unbuttoned and his arm on top of the door.

"Sonia, Sonia come on in. Would you like a drink?"

"I came to talk to Lucy," said Sonia as she walked over to the sofa and sat down. The record player had two records stacked on it and the needle kept bumping against the end of the record. Just above it was Francisco's and Lucy's wedding picture.

"She's in Connecticut. Remember?"

"Oh…. I forgot."

"Sure you did." He pulled out an album of boleros by Daniel Santos, held it by the edges between his hands, and blew on it to make sure that it would play smoothly. He placed the needle on the record and then sat next to Sonia.

"Why are you here, Sonia? You know that Lucy's visiting her sister. You know, I saw the way you were checking me out when I was dancing the other night." He started putting his arm around her.

"Slow down. I did come to see you, but not for that."

"For what then?"

Sonia hesitated. "Look. Forget it. I made a mistake." She got up thinking about Lucy's happiness now that Francisco had stopped associating with certain people and elements.

Francisco stopped her and asked her to sit back down.

"I'm curious. At least tell me what's up," he said.

"I need a gun." Sonia told him, and Francisco stood up straight with his eyes popped and his mouth, slightly open.

"Wow. You? For what?"

"Protection."

"From what or who?"

"Can you get it or not?" Sonia cut right to the chase.

"Yeah. I still know some people."

"By when?"

"Next week, same night. Meet me at the Victory at 7."

"Victory? Hotel? I don't know Frankie."

"That's right. You want it don't you?"

"Just the gun, Frankie. That's all I want."

And the night had come for Sonia to meet him. After delaying at work as much as she could, she left and took the bus to the hotel. She stood in front of the broken lights of the hotel sign that read, "Victor otel." Looking up she noticed each brick and for the first time thought about the beauty of the building's facade. The box fans in some of the windows, along with the silhouettes of women taking off their street wigs, to feel more comfortable in the performance of a sexual act gave an indication of the erotic tension deemed as criminal that was going on inside. She decided right at that moment that she would have to get what she came for, regardless of the price. The faint smell of urine hit her the minute she walked through the entrance. At the reception desk stood a white businessman wearing a fedora and blue suit. He was paying for a room and by his side stood a black woman about three inches taller than him with high heels wearing a short skirt and a low-cut blouse. She was fanning herself in an exaggerated motion. The clerk finished checking them in then handed the key to the man in a very cold and business like manner.

"Room 402," said Sonia to the clerk.

"Elevator's broke. Take those stairs up." He pointed to his right, while barely acknowledging her. Ordinarily she would have let a person know that she was not one to be dismissed but in this case, it suited her just fine.

Once she made it to the room, there was Francisco, true to his word. He was dressed for the occasion and had on just the right amount of cologne for Sonia's taste.

"You made it." He slowly walked up to her and smoothly brushed her hair away from her face and lightly touched her cheek with his fingers.

"Do you have the gun?" asked Sonia as she took his hand, held it, and placed it back on his side. Before letting go of his arm, she passed her hand along his tricep. She started breathing just a little faster. She felt a strange, inexplicable rush over getting this gun. This feeling combined with the attraction that she had always felt for Francisco had her leaning closer to him. At that moment, she decided to take control of the situation. She took a hold of his face and passionately kissed him. This action caught him off guard. He just stood there silent. Then Sonia stopped and stepped back and thought about Lucy and how she had been so kind to her. When Sonia was taking night classes at the community college she could leave Miguel Angel and Marisol with Lucy and she cared for them like the children that she never had. She would cook for them, help them with their homework and love them just as Sonia would.

"No. I can't do this. Not to Lucy." Sonia stepped further away from Francisco and sat on the other side of the bed.

Having regained his composure, Francisco walked over to her, sat down and started massaging her shoulders while telling her that everything was alright.

"Stop. Do you have the gun?" she interrupted him.

"Yeah. $200." Francisco pulled out the revolver and showed it to her.

She took it, pulled out the cylinder, took out the bullets and put each one back in less than five seconds. She held it, and felt the weight, and then stretched out her arm as if she was taking aim at a target.

He stood at her side, in shock.

"Damn, Sonia. Where'd you learn how to do all that?"

"My father. He had one for protection against anybody who would try to rob his store. So, he taught me for when I had to be there alone. You got this from your cousin?"

"That's right. Shorty can get you anything."

Sonia went into her purse pulled out the money and gave it to him.

"Listen Frankie, this is nobody's business. Understand?"

"Understood"

Sonia put the gun in her purse and walked out of the room.

"Look at Sinbad so big and strong, sitting like a king on his throne. They brought him here when he was just a baby. Even if he was free, he wouldn't even know how to live in the jungle." Valentina was talking about a majestic lowland gorilla.

The sun was shining in a blue sky, not a cloud in sight. Teachers could be heard reminding students to keep up and stay with the group as they walked from exhibit to exhibit on their end-of-the-year field trips.

Marisol looked at Valentina and wondered why she loved coming to this huge animal prison in which creatures who were meant to roam free in the wild were kept in steel cages, and a truck tire chained to the ground was supposed to be some type of amusement.

"Thanks for coming with me today," said Valentina. "You know that park down there, just south of the farm animals right before you get to the lake?" Valentina pointed towards a wide open space with grass that led to sand and the waves of the lake coming in and hitting the man-made shore line.

"Sophomore year my boyfriend and me had our own little picnic there," continued Valentina. "He was my first. Like a little fool I made us some sandwiches and brought some orange juice. And, of course, he didn't bring anything. He just had to show up. It was a little cool that day and the wind was hitting our faces as we sat on the grass and ate. Then that little chump says, "It would really be good to have some chips with these."

"Chips? He said that?" replied Marisol.

"He did. I didn't tell him he was an ingrate. I just agreed with him. But that was alright because even though I didn't say what was really on my mind, right then and there, I knew that I wasn't going to be cooking and cleaning for any man, any time soon."

Valentina and Marisol slapped each other five while laughing.

"When you were a little girl, do you ever remember your aunts and uncles asking you when are you going to get married?" asked Valentina.

"All the time. But mami would always answer for me and tell them how in the world would a little girl know that."

To the delight of the children who got right up as close as they could to the glass separating them from the gorillas, a mother gorilla groomed her baby while another held hers tight by the neck.

Valentina and Marisol kept on walking and then sat down at a bench in front of the seals, that were diving and swimming underwater then coming up to catch the sun and lay on the rocks.

"Hey, you want some?" Marisol got up and bought two bags of popcorn.

"I love this popcorn. Thanks Mari."

"Remember that musician from the other night?" asked Marisol.

"The sax player?"

"Who else? Yeah. He saw me at the library and tried talking to me."

"That fine ass guy tried talking to you? What did you do?"

"Nothing."

Valentina looked at Marisol with a bit of a surprised expression on her face.

"And guess what? He knows my brother," added Marisol.

"Is that what stopped you from getting to know him?" asked Valentina with a playful look of mock sexual desire in her eyes.

"No. I actually like the sound of his voice and he seems to be kind of sweet, but I don't want to be just another prize that he wins over."

"Why not, girl? Have some fun with him and if he wants to leave so what. This ain't 1930, baby."

"You can do that, Valentina, but I can't."

"What are you going to do the next time you see him? Guys like Omar have a rap for every situation."

"I don't know."

All of the sudden, Valentina was almost fixated by the sound of the seals as they dove off of the rocks and splashed into the water. Marisol noticed this and decided to stay silent.

"Gamaliel use to love going down to watch the seals swim underwater," said Valentina.

Marisol then understood why this place was so special to Valentina. She put her arm around Valentina and let her know that she was there for her.

"Mari, you may not see me around for a little while."

"What do you mean? You going somewhere?"

"I can't tell you but I just want you to know that I'll be alright."

Marisol wondered why Valentina was being so cryptic, but she also did not want to invade her privacy. Especially when she was feeling so vulnerable.

"Valentina, if you ever need anything, please just let me know."

"Don't worry. I'll be fine."

Marisol noticed that Valentina had lost some weight and had on a long sleeved blouse. She couldn't remember the last time that she had seen Valentina in short sleeves. Outside of Sonia, Valentina was one of the few people who appreciated and saw Marisol's talent and beauty. This meant a great deal to Marisol, and she left the zoo that day worried about what Valentina could have meant.

"It feels so good to cook for you two. It's a long time since we ate dinner together," said Sonia as she served the Friday night meal of cod fish with sweet potatoes and yucca.

"It's only been like two weeks mami" said Marisol.

"That's a long time. You'll understand when you have kids of your own."

The doorbell rang and Miguel Angel got up to go downstairs and open the door.

"That's my friend Omar," said Miguel Angel as he descended the stairs.

"Migue, what did I tell you about inviting people with out letting me know? What if I didn't cook enough?"

Hearing that the surprise guest was Omar, Marisol dashed straight to her room and fixed her hair only a little bit and then came back to the table and sat down.

"Don't worry ma, He didn't come to eat," said Miguel Angel. He walked in with Omar and introduced him.

"This is Omar," said Miguel Angel, pointing at Sonia.

"Hola, Señora. Omar Burgos at your service." Omar put his hand to his heart while shaking Sonia's hand.

"Sonia Concepción, un placer. Your friend is a true gentleman Migue. Please sit and join us."

"We're going out" said Miguel Angel.

Omar looked over at Marisol and instantly remembered her from the library.

"We have a little bit of time." He said as he sat down across from her.

"This is my sister Marisol."

"Marisol. That's a lovely name. I bet you love to hang out at the library."

"She does. How did you know?" asked Miguel Angel.

"He saw me there last week," Marisol answered for Omar.

Sonia got up and walked to the kitchen then came back with a plate for Omar.

"Wow. Some home cooked bacalao and verdura, muchas gracias Señora Concepción," said Omar before taking his first bite.

"This is delicious. I haven't had food like this since getting here from New York. Don't get me wrong. The restaurants here are good but there's nothing like the food that mami makes. Right Migue?"

"Yeah, yeah, I'm gonna go get ready" said Miguel Angel.

"Where are you two going?" asked Sonia.

"To Paradise," said Omar.

"Excuse me. I'll be right back," said Sonia.

"That's that club on the north side," said Marisol.

"Sure is. Want to join us?" asked Omar as he looked right at Marisol.

"Thank you but no. I'm not into that."

"Not into having a good time?" asked Omar, regaining some of the composure that he had lost at the library.

"What brings you to Chicago, Omar?" asked Sonia from the hallway as she was walking back from the kitchen, with a pot of coffee on a silver tray.

"I'm here to help my cousin with an album he's recording."

"Help him how?"

"I'm playing on it."

"A musician, that can be a hard life," said Sonia.

"True, but I love it. Sharing my songs with people, making them laugh, dance and even cry is a beautiful thing Señora Concepción."

The aroma of freshly brewed strong coffee added to the feeling of comfort that permeated the living room. Sonia had placed the red tablecloth that she only used for special occasions and holidays. Yes Marisol was right it had been only two weeks since they had shared dinner together but this was a way of Sonia slowing down the clock, hoping, praying, that if Miguel Angel had more time, he would come to his senses. And if this didn't work, she was determined to do anything to keep her son safe.

Omar's presence added to the tranquility created by Sonia. He told them about his playing the congas with his uncles and father at the age of three in Ponce, Puerto Rico.

"Your cousin told you about how Migue can fix any problem with your car?" asked Sonia.

"That's right. Your son's a genius," Omar said, turning his body and saying it loud enough for Miguel Angel to hear him.

"Marisol is talented as well," said Sonia.

"Really? What is this talent, Marisol?" asked Omar.

Before Marisol could say anything Sonia said, "Poetry. Go sit down in the living room. We can have some coffee and Mari can share a poem with us." Sonia poured the coffee, and a light steam came from the four cups.

"Maybe some other time" said Marisol. She wasn't feeling shy. She was more than confident, sitting up straight but not rigid. She felt that her current, separate pieces, were going to become one. She had ideas of combining the places, people and emotions into a flowing piece, that she would then share with an audience.

They started taking sips of their coffee while Sonia continued getting to know Omar, and she became more impressed with the polite and warm respectful way in which he spoke and carried himself.

"My aunt has the same one at her house," said Omar painting to the painting of The Last Supper hanging from the wall.

"People still praying to a blonde hair blue eyed Jesus hard to believe," said Marisol.

"That's your new crazy friend Valentina talking not you," said Sonia.

"Miguel Angel," called Sonia. "Why don't you bring us your guitar so that Omar can sing us a song." She quickly changed the subject not wanting to spoil the evening by getting into an argument with Marisol.

Miguel Angel came walking from his room dressed in clothes that resembled Omar's sense of style, black pleaded pants and a blue shirt underneath a black leather jacket. He bent over and kissed Sonia good bye, saying, "Bendición." For even if he was tired of telling Sonia that he was no longer a little boy who didn't need her protection, he would never dream of leaving home without asking for his mother's blessing.

"Dios te bendiga hijo."

"You can sing for us next time you come Omar" said Marisol.

"I'll sing and you read us some of your lines. Deal?"

Omar thanked Sonia for the meal that reminded him of home and his family, got up, and placed his cup on the dining room table. Then he and Miguel Angel left for Club Paradise. When they were in the car, Miguel Angel turned on his eight track and they were listening to Maurice White sing "That's the Way of the World."

"Man, these cat's can play!" said Omar, as he launched into an explanation of the instrumental genius behind the music.

Miguel Angel was tapping a rhythm on the steering wheel and bopping his head to the beat. "Yeah. They're cool."

They came to a red light and Miguel turned to face Omar.

"You like my sister," said Miguel Angel.

Omar was caught a little off guard. He didn't see how Miguel Angel was able to make that observation having spent so little time in the same room with them.

"I don't really know her," answered Omar.

"I saw how you were looking at her."

"Sorry I didn't mean to be disrespectful Migue. But she is beautiful."

"That's alright. Just be cool."

"I will. But tonight this is all about you remember?"

"Racing, right," said Miguel Angel as they drove north on Lake Shore drive.

"You got it, brother. Just tell the ladies how your heart starts beating fast before a race, and how you have to handle the steering wheel but not hold on to it too tight, when you step on the gas and keep the car moving in the right direction. You'll have them falling for you big time. Trust me."

The pulsating lights and smoke coming from the floor enveloped the dancers as they moved to intoxicating sounds from the DJ booth. Most of them had their eyes closed, hypnotized by whatever reality they were imagining for the night. Straight, gay, black, white, latino, they all came together here and created a fantasy of equality that lasted until five in the morning. Then they would all go back to take their place in the hierarchy that gave them power or stripped them of their humanity depending on their assigned status.

Miguel Angel and Omar sat down at a table near the center facing the dance floor. The waitress brought over a couple of drinks then winked at Omar and placed her soft lips on his cheek, before going to wait on another table. He took a napkin and wiped off the red lipstick while looking sheepishly at Miguel Angel.

"Just a friend," said Omar, remembering their conversation about Marisol.

"None of my business," said Miguel Angel, looking straight ahead at the dance floor.

"Cool." Omar felt a little relieved in knowing that Miguel Angel would not go talking to Marisol about anything that he heard or saw tonight. It was as if they had an implicit deal that in exchange for Omar giving away his smooth secrets on how to be a Casanova, Miguel Angel would stay silent.

Omar pointed at two women who had just walked in. One was smoking a cigarette and had on a creme-colored dress and the other a red blouse with blue jeans.

"See those two girls right there?" said Omar.

"Yeah"

"They're looking for a place to sit, and that's just what we're going to give them. Now when I come back with them, be a perfect gentleman."

Omar got up and walked over to them flashing his confident and charming smile. He whispered into the ear of the women in the jeans while looking back at Miguel Angel sitting at the table. The three of them walked back to the table together.

"Miguel Angel, say hello to Dora and Linda," said Omar loudly over the music.

Miguel Angel got up and offered them two chairs at the table.

The song "There But For the Grace of God Go I," came on as a few dancers left the dance floor while others took the chance to fill the open space.

"These lyrics are so deep" said Omar to Dora. She looked at him with a blank stare, and for a second, in his mind he saw, Marisol sitting at the library surrounded by books and getting ready to stand up and look for more knowledge.

"The song, it's cool" Omar made another effort to connect.

Dora answered, "Cool beat."

"So you two girls are waitresses at the place up the street?" asked Omar as Miguel Angel, trying to hide his being nervous by moving to the beat, looked on, waiting for his cue from Omar.

Omar didn't get his chance. Linda noticed that even if Miguel Angel wasn't comfortable, he had a good sense of rhythm and coordination. She had also seen his well-toned body when he got up and this combination was more than enough for her. Her man was one year into serving a seven-year prison sentence and she didn't plan on waiting another six years. She told Dora to order her a vodka and cranberry juice then took Miguel Angel by the hand, and led him to the dance floor.

Miguel Angel looked at the other couples dancing and just did his best to keep up with Linda who was in a hypnotic trance. She turned her back to him and pressed up against his body while taking his arms and putting them around her waist.

Miguel Angel took the opportunity to say his rehearsed lines.

They kept dancing, and Linda felt a little bead of sweat on her forehead. She motioned to Miguel Angel that she was getting tired, and they walked back to their table.

"Dora, he races cars," Linda said to her friend while swallowing nearly half of her drink.

"Cars?" said Dora.

Omar looked at Miguel Angel and winked. The night was going just as he had planned, with the exception of his not being able to stop thinking about Marisol.

After a few more drinks and a little bit more of dancing they found themselves in Miguel Angel's car on the way to Dora's apartment on the other side of the city. Right before getting on Lake Shore Drive, Miguel Angel revved up the engine and stepped on the gas. It was as if the lake was moving right past them and the rest of the cars were standing still. He didn't hold on to the steering wheel too tightly. and the windows were down just enough for them to feel the wind.

Once they got to Dora's place, Miguel Angel and Linda stayed in the living room while Omar and Dora found their way to her bedroom.

Dora planted her full lips on his mouth and kissed him slowly, gently pulling his lips forward. She walked over to her dresser, struck a match and lit a vanilla-scented candle. They put their arms around each other and with one smooth motion, their bodies fell in sync on to her bed.

Omar felt the mattress undulating on his back.

"A waterbed," he whispered in her ear.

"Like it, right, baby?"

"Yeah," he said as he kissed her neck. In reality he didn't care for it, but he wanted to stay in the moment, which with each passing second was becoming harder for him to do. For some strange reason he was thinking about the night he played at the Cultural Center with his cousin's band. He could see himself on stage delighting the people with his sax solo, and although he only thought about music during a performance, in this vision he also saw himself wondering where in the audience was Marisol.

He stopped kissing Dora, and asked where was the bathroom. She pointed and he walked over to it, closed the door and started looking at himself in the mirror.

Meanwhile, Linda and Miguel Angel were on the living room sofa, and he was trying his best to hide the fact that he was nervous. He had only been with one woman, his first girlfriend Cristina, which was about two years ago.

Linda took total control and unzipped his pants, placing her hand inside. She felt him getting hard and harder, then she got up, slipped out of her panties, and sat on him.

"Ohhhh," moaned Linda. "Yessss"

Miguel Angel was trying his best to not get overly excited, but he couldn't help what was about to happen. His body shook for a second, and he let out a sound that was a cross between a moan and a whimper. Then he was perfectly still.

"Keep going, don't stop," said Linda, hoping he could continue. "No man, you ain't racing now."

"Sorry," was all that Miguel Angel could say.

She got up, put on her panties and jeans then lit a cigarette. A few minutes later Omar came out of the bedroom with a disappointed Dora behind him. He couldn't remember this ever happening to him, but after having had sex that was solely based on a physical attraction, he felt guilty.

"Hey Migue let's go."

"Now? You just got here," said Dora.

"No, they can go," Linda said in between a puff of her cigarette.

CHAPTER 8

"That's the last time I clean that old lady's shit!" said Mr. Curtis as he slammed a bottle of Pine Sol into his bucket. He was a janitor at The Manor, a 50-unit assisted living home. Here the residents gave up the freedom to cook and eat whatever they wanted in exchange for a menu that was forced on them and that restricted anything and everything worth eating.

"Sorry Mr. Curtis. She doesn't mean any harm," Marisol tried explaining to Mr. Curtis what he already knew. If Mrs. Marlowe could not control her bowel movements she was going to have to live in a full-blown nursing home and that idea terrified Mrs. Marlowe. Marisol was protecting Mrs. Marlowe from the inevitable.

"Better tell her Marisol, one more time, just...." He turned his back, walked down the hall, and opened the door to the stairway.

Marisol used her key to open the door.

"Mrs. Marlowe? Hello....?" Marisol did not hear an answer.

"Mrs. Marlowe...." Marisol walked into Mrs. Marlowe's bedroom looked in the mirror of the dresser and saw Mrs. Marlowe, kneeling, hiding."

"Come on, Mrs. Marlowe. It's alright." Marisol extended her hand, and Mrs. Marlowe grabbed on to it tightly, slightly shaking.

"A man in the dining room," she said in a barely audible whisper with her finger over her lips and pointing at the dining room, begging Marisol not to give up their location.

"Shhh. The man in the dining room," repeated Mrs. Marlowe.

"I didn't see a man Mrs. Marlowe" said Marisol, assuring her there was no man sitting in the dining room waiting for her.

When they walked over, Mrs. Marlowe pointed to a black fedora that was on her table. It had belonged to her son Stanley, who hadn't visited her in three years. She had forgotten that she had spent the two last hours just holding and staring at the hat, wondering when he was going to come back for it. When she came back and saw it on top of her chair, she thought that a man had broken in and was sitting at the table waiting for her.

"See, nothing to worry about," said Marisol. "It's just a hat."

"Oh. I'm such an old fool," said Mrs. Marlowe as she looked at the floor.

"Forget about that. I brought you your favorite chocolate eclairs from the bakery. Sit and I'll make some coffee."

"Oh, my dear Marisol. What would I do without you?"

Mrs. Marlowe relaxed. She sat in her rocking chair, put on her reading glasses, and started reading the newspaper Marisol had brought for her.

"Robbery, mugging, another politician on trial for bribery, don't know why I bother." Mrs. Marlowe, disgusted with the headlines, just let the paper hang from her hands and started rocking with her head back, humming Glenn Miller's "Moonlight Serenade."

"Marisol..... have you made up your mind?" asked Mrs. Marlowe.

"Made up my mind?"

"UCLA. Are you going?"

Marisol had gotten accepted into the university last year but had decided to take a year off from school. She didn't feel ready to leave her home and most of all did not want to burden Sonia with any additional expenses.

Marisol sat on the sofa next to Mrs. Marlowe. "I don't know."

"But you must go dear. Your mind will flourish there. You could even study abroad in Paris or Madrid. See Europe, see the world."

"I have been thinking more about it lately Mrs. Marlowe."

Marisol took a sip of coffee and a bite of her eclair, looked at Mrs. Marlowe, and smiled.

"There is something a little bit different about you today. Is that a new outfit?" asked Mrs. Marlowe.

Marisol was wearing a new powder blue blouse and red skirt.

"Do you have a new friend dear?" asked Mrs. Marlowe with a smile as she gently put her hand on Marisol's shoulder.

"I do. He's meeting me here," said Marisol, blushing. "He really is just a friend."

"Tell me about him. Is he a good young man?." Mrs. Marlowe trusted Marisol's judgement but she wanted to hear about Marisol's new found joy. She was hoping that if it was only a friendship, that it wouldn't take long for it to blossom into a beautiful romance.

"We met at the library and he's a friend of my brother's," said Marisol.

"Does he work, go to school?"

"He's a musician." As soon as Marisol said it she saw the doubt in Mrs. Marlowe's eyes. Mrs. Marlowe rocked back slightly in her chair, then sat up just a little closer to Marisol. True to her way of being, Mrs. Marlowe showed concern without being judgmental.

"Tell me more," said Mrs. Marlowe.

"The first time I saw him he was playing with his cousin's band at the Betances Cultural Center. The sounds that came out of his saxophone were so beautiful."

"So they finished playing, you were mesmerized, and stared at him. Then he came over to talk to you straight from the stage right?"

"No, we didn't even talk that night. The next time I saw him was at the library. He is from New York and is here to help his cousin with an album they're recording."

"Sounds like an ambitious young man."

Mrs. Marlowe got up from her chair and walked over to her window. The sound of her slippers dragging on the floor was a stark contrast to the vibrant steps that Marisol remembered hearing when Mrs. Marlowe walked quickly on the wooden floor in between the rows of desks going from one student to the next. She had been the first teacher who had not admonished her for wearing her winter hat in the classroom. Instead, she talked to her in a soft tone about how beautiful she would be if she took it off and sat up straight like a dignified young lady.

Marisol heard keys opening the door and turned to see Mrs. Marlowe's aide, Stephanie. She had been taking care of her for three months now. Her brown roots came out from the middle of her head, trying their best to blend in with her bleached blonde hair. Her patience with Mrs. Marlowe was starting to wear thin but she still managed to treat her as kindly as she possibly could.

"Hi, Stephanie." Marisol greeted Stephanie, then walked over to put her arm around Mrs. Marlowe."

"Mr. Curtis told me what you did. You gotta stop that. You're gonna ruin this beautiful rug, you keep that up," Stephanie said to Mrs. Marlowe, scolding her as if she were a child.

"She doesn't do that on purpose," said Marisol in defense of the woman who had encouraged her love of books, writing, and poetry.

"Don't let her fool you, Marisol. She knows what she's doin'" said Stephanie.

Mrs. Marlowe sat back in her chair and just looked at Stephanie while slowly rocking.

Marisol bent down and took Mrs. Marlowe's small hand into hers and said,

"I'll come back next week. Call me if you need anything before that."

"UCLA. That's where you belong." Mrs. Marlowe gently touched Marisol's shoulder and kissed her cheek.

When Marisol got downstairs Omar was waiting for her and they walked a few blocks to the Blue Garden Chinese restaurant.

"That's some pretty nice sized shrimp in that rice. How is it?" asked Omar.

"I wonder if the same cook is working today. It taste just a little different," answered Marisol. "Why would you order a T-bone steak in a Chinese place?"

"It was on the menu and I like steak," replied Omar.

Marisol liked coming here because from every table you could see the people walking past the front of the restaurant. Even as a little girl she would make up stories about them, the men who came stumbling drunk out of the bar a half block away, the children who were trying to skip and walk as fast as they could on their way to play baseball or basketball or just to fly on the swings, and the lovers holding hands and walking as slowly as possible, savoring every second of their romance. Marisol had a story for all of them.

"Your mom seems pretty cool," said Omar smiling at Marisol and leaning forward wanting to know more about her. "How about your pops?" he asked.

"I loved him.."

"Loved?"

"He died in a car accident," said Marisol. She continued eating her shrimp fried rice but just a little slower.

"That's cool. We don't need to talk about him."

Marisol slowly put down her fork and took out a picture of her, on her father's lap when she was three years old. She was wearing a pink sweater, black pants, and a big smile, her head and hair pressed against her father's chest. He was beaming with love and pride for his special little girl.

"When he would take me to the park and push me on the swings, I felt like I could touch the sky. Every time we went, he was just about the only man there and that's why he hated Father's Day. He called all the men who showed up only once a year big phonies. On that day the only man that he talked to was the piraguero. We loved to order piraguas de coco and hear the shaved ice coming off the huge block on the cart. That coco flavored ice would feel so good going down after playing on the swings and running from my father chasing me, pretending to be a monster."

"Seems like he was a good man. Knowing you and Miguel Angel I bet that your parents really got along," said Omar.

"They used to look so beautiful dancing together. She loved the way he moved and how he spun her. All of this changed when he started to gamble. I even heard him crying one night, sitting on his bad after drinking some beer and Canadian whiskey. His head was down, and he looked up at me when he noticed that I was standing in the hallway looking through the open door. He said, 'I'm sick mama, I'm sick.' Then he closed the door and told me to go with my mother and I heard his sobbing become louder. The car accident only finished killing my father. Who he really was had already died a slow death."

The rain started coming down one drop at a time on the front window of the restaurant. Then the clouds opened up and the people walking outside went underneath the awnings along the avenue, hoping that the rain would not last too long.

"After he died, mami finished raising Miguel Angel and I on her own."

"She's a strong woman, your mother."

"What about you, music man? Tell me more about you," said Marisol.

"I can tell you about that the next time we get together."

"So, you know there's going to be a next time?"

'Well, will you go out with me again Marisol?" said Omar as he took her hand and kissed it.

"Yes," answered Marisol.

They finished their lunch and walked out into the rain not caring that they didn't have umbrellas.

A bee was buzzing around the flowers. "You're too close. It's going to sting" said Sonia to Father Alberto as she saw him bend over to touch the false indigo growing in the garden behind the rectory.

"She doesn't want anything from me. She's coming for nectar, and the flower is calling it," said Father Alberto. He had a keen sense of when a situation was truly dangerous that had been honed by watching soldiers coming on Jeeps, brandishing their weapons to poor farmers and people who worked the land in El Salvador. With time, just by looking at the soldiers' eyes, he knew when they were coming merely to intimidate versus when they were coming to kill and torture those who were, according to them, hiding guerrillas.

"I've never been back here," said Sonia to Father Alberto. There was a part of her that felt a bit uncomfortable being in such a romantic place on a lovely sunny day with a handsome man who happened to be a priest.

"Beautiful isn't it?" Father Alberto continued talking to Sonia as he watered the beautiful purple and green flowers that had come into full bloom.

"I can come some other time," said Sonia.

"Stay. Let me give you my full attention. Please sit."

They walked over to a small round table in the middle of the garden. He poured water from a silver colored pitcher into two glasses and let her know that he was ready and willing to listen to her.

"Tell me, what is troubling you?" He spoke in a way that demonstrated a subtle and soft yet incredibly strong will to care for his people.

"My son Miguel Angel.."

"Marisol has talked about him a few times, although I know your daughter much better through Valentina from the Betances Center."

"How is that girl? I haven't heard Marisol say anything about her lately."

"She's fine. You were saying something about Miguel Angel." Father Alberto quickly changed the subject.

"At work, I am so distracted, leaving messages for the wrong people, forgetting appointments, and making other mistakes more often."

Sonia paused for a moment and looked up at the few puffy clouds against the backdrop of a blue sky. For her they formed a ladder that went higher and higher. This allowed her to briefly escape, as she did not want to divulge what she was about to say.

"I can't get out of my mind how I recently spent time in a run-down hotel room with a man who is my dear friend's husband..." said Sonia.

"Did you..."

"No I didn't," said Sonia, answering the sexual question that absolutely meant nothing to her. She continued talking while looking past father Alberto in the direction of the rectory. "I met him there to buy a gun."

"A gun?"

"Yes. There is a part of me feeling that I started losing my soul, the day I came to this country. Palm trees and sugar cane turned into snow when we got off that plane."

"You need this gun to protect yourself," said Father Alberto.

Sonia decided that she could no longer hold in the thought of using the revolver on Big Angel. She had come to peace with the idea that she would take a life, if it meant protecting her son.

"I am thinking about killing a man, Father," Sonia said softly. Then she started to cry.

Father Alberto pulled out his handkerchief and handed it to her.

"Why? Why would you even need to do that?"

"This world can have my soul but it will not do the same to my children. I will protect them until the day that I can no longer. That day is up to God, and only God."

Father Alberto witnessed the killing of his friends and fellow priests in El Salvador because they had the audacity to preach the gospels as instruments of liberation for the poor, and marginalized. People having to make a choice between becoming active soldiers in a war or watching their families starve to death and live under conditions designed to debilitate and destroy the very essence of their humanity, was nothing new to him. Under these circumstances Father Alberto felt the despair and anguish of his flock. It pained him to know that Sonia had come to the point of feeling that she needed to kill a man.

Sonia continued telling Father Alberto how when her son was a child she had always encouraged Miguel Angel's spending time at the park swimming pool and was his biggest supporter when he had diving competitions. She knew that as long as he was getting praise for this he would have no need to find himself in a gang like so many of her friends' sons. There was Romana Garcia's son, Timoteo who was known as 'Smiley' on the street and could be found outside of that same pool selling nickel and dime bags. Smiley did that until one summer day in July when two kids from a rival gang came out of nowhere and drilled three shots in his chest.

And now that Miguel Angel was on his way to becoming an independent man all of Sonia's sacrifices would be for nothing if he was going to work for Big Angel.

"Sonia. You do not want to take a man's life. Not you. Not here," said Father Alberto. "What has this man done?"

"He runs a 'legit' business that allows him to run gambling, stolen goods, and whatever else brings him way more money than his legal business. He will not hesitate to kill anyone who interferes with his work," answered Sonia.

"What has he done to you?" asked Father Alberto.

"This man wants my son to work for him when he opens up his new shop. He claims that Miguel Angel won't be in any danger. But you know so often it is the innocent who pay the price."

"Your son, he wants to do this?"

"Yes. We argue because he claims.. that he knows what he's doing. 'I'm a man,' he tells me."

"He is, Sonia. The more that you tell him to stay away from this man and this opportunity, the more he will want to do it. He wants to live his life freely," said Father Alberto.

"I know. That is why I have come to this conclusion. It may be the only way to save my son," said Sonia with a resolve that let Father Alberto know that she meant every word.

"You have raised him well. It's possible that you may just have to be there for him when things go wrong. And things will go wrong, no matter what he chooses. There is nothing that we can do about that. Let him live his life. What good will you be to him in prison or God forbid dead?

Oscar walked into Big Angel's office and saw a stranger sitting behind his desk. The man and Big Angel were finishing up a conversation and he stood up to shake Big Angel's hand. As the stranger was leaving Oscar noticed his musk oil cologne and that this unannounced visitor was at least two inches shorter than Big Angel.

"Who was that?" asked Oscar.

"One of Conglese's new guys. He was just here to make sure the numbers are adding up for their cut. Especially now that Shorty Suarez gave us a piece of Salsero.

Shorty Suarez was a club owner who never met a dice game that he didn't like." He was in to Big Angel for about ten thousand dollars with absolutely no way of paying it back. So he cut him on the money being made at one of the hottest salsa dance places in town.

"Why was he sitting in your chair? asked Oscar.

"He was there when I came in. As if I needed a reminder that the Italians don't play. Said he'd be back next week."

Big Angel sat back down and took a bottle of JB scotch from the cabinet next to his desk. He poured a drink for himself and another for Oscar. It wasn't the first time that he had received a visit from the Italians, but he also knew that the minute they had any suspicion that he was holding on to their money, they would be back. A man like him was only used to intimidating people as opposed to being on the receiving end. This visit by Conglese's new enforcer just reminded him of who was truly in charge when it came to illegal business in this city. His dice games were making more money these days and he knew it would only be a matter of time before they started demanding a bigger piece of the pie.

Oscar took a shot of scotch. "Man it burns going down, but it's good! Hey man..uh... uh.... I don't wanna tell you but.. uh... that lady is back," said Oscar.

"What lady?"

"You know, the kid's mother."

"Again. What a pain in the ass."

Considering recent developments Big Angel felt like he needed Miguel Angel now more than ever. He needed to insulate himself with people he could trust and he trusted Miguel Angel even more than Oscar.

"Damn. How many times do I have to tell this lady the same thing?" said Big Angel. "Alright, go tell her that she can come on up." He quickly passed his comb through his hair and straightened his shirt, remembering the lessons that his father taught him about always looking sharp.

Sonia walked in and saw the bottle of scotch on the desk.

"Wanna drink?" asked Big Angel.

"Yes please" answered Sonia, wanting to connect with him. She noticed that her acceptance caught Big Angel a bit off guard, but he recovered smoothly and poured into a paper cup.

"Only the finest cups, for you Señora Concepción."

Sonia took the cup, thanked him, and sat down. She took a sip of her drink and politely put it down, letting him know that it wasn't of the highest quality. Mr. Reynolds being a connoisseur of single malt scotch, had introduced it to her at some of the company Christmas parties.

"A man in your position deserves a better drink," said Sonia. Hearing this, Big Angel reclined in his chair and smiled.

Sonia was feeling the weight of the gun in her purse on her lap. Then she touched it, preparing herself for the reality of possibly ending this man's life. Then after an awkward silence in which the sound of the tire bolts being turned and removed from cars became louder, Big Angel started talking again.

"You're here about your son again, right?"

"Yes. Your mother would have done the same for you, I'm sure."

"She never got the chance. She died when I was nine."

"I'm sorry Mr. Cintron."

"Why? It wasn't your fault that some punk shot her even though she gave him her purse."

For the first time Sonia saw vulnerability in Big Angel. He never showed this to her or anyone else. She was conflicted by the sympathy that she was feeling for a man she knew was capable of committing murder if anybody dared to take what was his.

"Mr. Cintron you know why I am here today but I will let you get back to your business as you call it." Sonia took her hand away from her purse and the gun inside of it. In the back of her mind she also remembered that on nights when she couldn't sleep, she had seen Big Angel come out of his shop alone many times at midnight, one or two in the morning. If she was going to go through with this that would be a much more opportune time.

"I will come back soon, Mr. Cintron to talk to you about my son. Take care for now," said Sonia as she stood up and started to walk out of his office.

"Hold on a second." Big Angel looked at her and thought that these were the first pair of eyes that looked at him with honesty today. Upon hearing about his mother being killed, she showed compassion for him despite the fact that she had hatred in heart for him.

"Señora Concepción why don't you join me for a drink?"

Sonia looked at him almost in shock not knowing what to say.

"And it would be one of those places in Old Town where they have classy scotch," said Big Angel. "What do you say?"

"Why do you want to have a drink with me?" asked Sonia, doubting his motives.

"Don't know really. I just know that I need to get away from here and you're standing there. So........" That was the best he could say without letting her know that he felt that he could be vulnerable around her. Or at least as vulnerable as circumstances would allow him to be.

Sonia felt that this might help her chances of Big Angel finally respecting her wishes. So she accepted the invitation.

Once they got to Sydney's Place they were able to find an outdoor table on this beautiful seventy-five degree night. Three men dressed in suits along with three women in their evening dresses were in contrast to the long-haired hippies who were loving the vibrant folk music scene. All kinds of people were attracted to this place for its eclectic nature.

"The usual Mr. Cintron?" asked the waiter.

"Yeah thanks Charlie." Replied Big Angel.

"And for the lady?" The waiter bowed slightly in Sonia's direction.

"A Manhattan please," said Sonia, making sure that the waiter looked at her and not Big Angel.

"I noticed that you didn't tell him to call you Big Angel."

"Like I said, I need to get away."

Sonia understood that he needed a rest from being on guard.

The waiter dressed in a traditional red jacket, white shirt and black tie brought them their drinks. They took a sip and just sat in silence for a few minutes. The sound of a car horn from an inpatient driver going south on Wells Street snapped them out of their way-too-brief respite.

"I have to tell you, you're a pretty lady," said Big Angel for the first time noticing the beauty of Sonia's short black wavy hair against her caramel-colored skin.

"I really don't know anything about you," Sonia answered him, not wanting to be rude but also not letting the conversation go in a romantic direction.

Big Angel saw a couple walk past them with a boy about the age of nine enjoying a piece of chocolate fudge from the candy store up the street.

"He looks the same age I was when I got here," said Big Angel.

"Chicago?"

"Yeah," he said, still looking at the family.

"That's when your mother...."

Big Angel began talking. He was feeling more and more at ease with Sonia.

"She wasn't killed by a punk, or a least one that wasn't a stranger." Big Angel moved the glass around in his hand then took another drink before putting it down, relaxing his shoulders and falling back into his chair.

"She knew the man," said Sonia.

"My old man, my father, he did it. He was a two bit numbers runner in the Bronx. My mother always used to say that he was different when they lived in Barranquitas back in Puerto Rico. Once they got to New York, he started hitting the booze heavy and thought he could lay his hands on mom whenever he needed to make a point."

Sonia looked at Big Angel lean forward in his chair, resembling a child who is crouching in fear. She put her hand on his.

"I remember how mom and me would be at home watching tv or eating and we would hear the front door slam. She didn't want me to worry but I always saw her eyes would open wide and she would send me to my room. To this day I can't stand to hear couples arguing, it makes me just want to tell them to shut the hell up before I shut them up. My father's screaming would get louder and louder until his hand would come down on her face. There I was a helpless kid balled up in my closet crying."

"Mr. Cintron you don't have to.." Sonia wanted to let him know that he didn't need to keep talking about this painful part of his life but Big Angel felt safe with Sonia and continued talking.

"One night he actually hit her with a balled-up fist. She hit her head against the radiator, was knocked unconscious, and never woke up. The bum is still in jail." Big Angel finished the story, sat up straight and finished his drink. It was strange, but when he sat up he had almost the same countenance and expression on his face that he had back at his garage.

"Why was he like that?" asked Sonia.

"He was a paranoid jealous drunk no good bastard. That's why."

"I am truly sorry Mr. Cintron."

"Don't be, you didn't do anything."

Riding back in Big Angel's car they felt the summer breeze coming in through the rolled down windows. As they passed the park, the baseball diamonds were empty. There weren't any kids running bases, hitting balls, or encouraging their friends to get a base hit. Instead, there were young couples walking hand in hand or sitting on the benches and sharing kisses.

When Big Angel stopped in front of Sonia's home, Miguel Angel and Omar were there also taking in the beautiful night and talking about the possibility of Miguel Angel racing his car next week. What started as a line to pick up women had turned into a reality that made him one hundred dollars or more a race.

Big Angel got out of the car and walked over to open the passenger door for Sonia and thanked her for her company and for listening to him. They both looked at Miguel Angel, who stood there with his mouth open in disbelief.

"Señora Concepción, thanks for tonight but —"

"I know, this changes nothing. You still want my son to work for you," said Sonia interrupting him before he had a chance to finish.

Sonia felt relieved and conflicted in knowing that by being there for Big Angel when he was in a vulnerable state, it would make it much easier to pull the trigger, and kill this man.

Big Angel turned to Miguel Angel and called him over.

"Migue come here, kid."

Miguel Angel walked to him slowly, still confused.

"Don't worry, kid, nothing's happening, just shared a drink, that's all. I gotta tell you one thing though, no more late night drag racing on Clybourn avenue. Got it?" said Big Angel, standing in front of Miguel Angel with his hand on his shoulder.

Miguel Angel felt the weight of Big Angel's arm and knew that there would be no negotiating on this.

"How did you know?" asked Miguel Angel.

"Come on. You know that sooner or later I find out about everything."

"But girls like it"

"Yeah, but they like money even more and you're gonna be making a lot with me. So, I can't risk you getting hurt over small potatoes. If you wanna impress some girl on a date, just let me know. I'll take care of you."

Big Angel tapped him lightly on this face, got into his car and drove off.

CHAPTER 9

*T*he following morning Marisol walked into the kitchen and found Miguel Angel sitting at the breakfast table eating and staring at their mother's empty chair. Sonia was at work early that morning to complete some of the new student enrollment reports for Mr. Reynolds.

Marisol sat down and served herself some of the scrambled eggs that Miguel Angel had prepared. She spread a little butter on a Kaiser roll and thanked him.

"She was with him last night," said Miguel Angel as he was still trying to process the thought of his mother spending time with Big Angel.

"Who is she and him?" By the way he was looking at where Sonia usually sits, Marisol had the feeling that he was talking about their mother, but didn't know who else he meant.

"Big Angel and mom," said Miguel Angel.

"What? Start from the beginning," Marisol said, surprised but not completely shocked by what he had just said.

"Me and Omar were out front, then his car pulled up, and mom got out" said Miguel Angel.

"You know she probably was with him, to talk about you."

Marisol knew that her mother had no romantic interest in Big Angel and that the only reason she would spend time with him would be to put an end to the idea of Miguel Angel working for him. The sound of the bus stopping in front of their building, picking up passengers to take them to work, came through their open window and reminded Marisol that she needed to get on with her day. After work, she planned on going by Valentina's as she hadn't seen her for a few weeks and she was beginning to worry.

"Don't worry about mom, Migue. You still plan on running Big Angel's new place?" asked Marisol.

Miguel Angel didn't say anything he just looked at her. He stopped tapping his fork on the now empty plate.

"I'm not gonna be fixing cars out of Mrs. Larsen's garage forever, Mari."

"I guess you know what you're doing." She kissed him on his forehead then went to finish getting ready for work.

She turned on the radio in her room and moved to the beat of her favorite songs while putting on her red bell bottom pants and plaid blouse. They were a gift from Olga the cashier. She had always encouraged Marisol to be a little bolder with her fashion.

Olga had absolutely no problems expressing all of her thoughts and shared even intimate details about her lovers. She dated married men who would buy her bracelets, earrings, and fine clothes. As she put it, she had hit the lottery with one of them, a retired attorney twenty years older who came to the flower shop to buy an arrangement marking his fortieth wedding anniversary. He became so infatuated with Olga that in exchange for her time and body he paid her rent for three months. That was when he found out that he wasn't the only one in Olga's bed. He was a fool who soon discovered that his money did not buy him control over her. She was a beautiful black Puerto Rican from Ponce who would tell Marisol, "Always walk straight with your held up high, negrita. That's right and whoever doesn't like it you just ignore them and keep right on walking."

When Marisol got to work that day she waved hello to Olga who was busy ringing up a customer. Olga pulled out three dollar bills and forty five cents from the register and handed them to the man.

"Love those pants Mari." said Olga as soon as the register drawer slid shut.

Marisol spent most of the day cutting flowers for three weddings that were happening next week. She worked with precision and detail, even though at times her thoughts would turn to Omar and their blooming relationship. She also thought about going to the Cultural Center and to Valentina's after work.

At lunch in the break room Olga and Marisol were eating when Olga pointed at the TV telling Marisol to turn around. Olga walked up and turned up the volume. It was a special report, and two bodies covered by white sheets were being carried out in stretchers from a National Guard armory. The bodies were independentistas who had broken in and were immediately killed by the guardsmen on duty, who thought that they were carrying weapons. The report was interrupted by the alert of oncoming thunderstorms for the area but Marisol missed this as she got up and walked quickly to the manager's office.

She immediately asked for the rest of the day off, and raced over to the Cultural Center, which was closed to the public but Marisol saw the cars parked in front.

The sky became increasingly gray as the sound of the first drops of rain hit the sidewalk, and the wind moved the tree branches in front of the building. Marisol was not deterred by the water, wind or any other obstacle. She needed to have information on Valentina, so she pounded on the doors with both hands.

"Open these doors now!" she yelled.

Juan Sanchez came running up the stairs and peered through the window, hardly able to make out who it was. He turned the lock and opened the door, letting her come in from the storm.

"Are you crazy? We're not open, why are you banging on the doors like that? Connie, Connie, please bring me a towel." Juan called to Connie, a cultural center member, as Marisol stood in front of him wiping the rain and tears from her eyes. Then he handed her the towel.

"Use this. Valentina isn't here."

The soft cotton against her face helped Marisol calm down. She asked if Valentina was still alive, fearing that she had been killed in the attack on the armory.

"Valentina isn't dead, but that's all I can tell you," said Juan with a steely look in his eyes. "I have to get back to our meeting. You can wait up here until it stops raining but then you have to go. We're going to be harassed by the FBI for the next few weeks or so. They are going to flip furniture and interrogate people. You don't want to be here for that."

"I need to see her, I need to know that she's alright." Marisol was just as determined as he was.

Standing in front of him in wet clothes and not at all concerned about anything other than her friend, Marisol embodied the discipline of a person would be a tremendous addition to the movement.

"If you come back in a couple of days, I might have some information for you, ok?" said Juan.

"Thank you." Marisol handed him back the towel and started walking out the door. She preferred walking in the heavy rain as opposed to feeling the pain of being at the Center without knowing anything about Valentina.

"Wait, you can't walk home in this. Saul.... come up here." called Juan.

An older gentleman came up and Juan asked him to give Marisol a ride home.

Once home, Marisol took a hot shower and changed into the comfort of her bath robe. For a few minutes she just sat on the sofa looking out of the window, wondering where she would go. Tomorrow she would be at work again and get lost digging into the soil with her bare hands and cutting edges of leaves to make lovely arrangements. Life would take over for two days, then she would have some news on Valentina. But at this very moment she needed the world to slow down, she needed the merry-go-round to slowly come to a stop, then she could lose herself in the tenderness of Omar's hands.

Marisol knew deep down that any time spent with Omar would be, at least for now temporary. She had made up her mind to accept the scholarship and attend UCLA in the fall. This did not coincide with Omar's musical plans, but it was time for Marisol to be truly liberated. But at this very moment, she longed to get lost in passion.

In spite of her wanting to stay neutral, she had been pulled into the tug of war between her mother and brother. She was overjoyed for her brother and the success that he had found as a wizard with engines. And yet she knew that her mother was right. It would only be a matter of time before Miguel Angel would be in over his head in a scenario that would not end pretty for him if he worked for Big Angel.

She held these thoughts about Valentina, her future and her family simultaneously. Then, the natural connection that she felt with Omar soothed her. She could be intimate with him simply because she wanted to share her body and essence. She didn't feel compelled to do it out of fear of not being accepted, because she didn't give in to the sexual whims of some kid with an erection.

She picked up the phone and called Omar letting the dial spin back slowly for all seven digits.

Marisol felt the callouses from playing guitar on Omar's hands as he gently squeezed her big toe before getting up to get her a glass of water. She loved that he had been careful and used the soft part of his palms to caress her breasts and legs, all the way from her ankles to her waist. The rhythm of his movements called her name when he took long deep strokes while inside of her. And she answered not with words but with sounds that he also made with her. They were in tune, playing a duet that was only for their ears.

She saw the box of condoms on his dresser and, was not surprised that there were only two left. She thought it funny that in his room, next to the framed posters of Ismael Rivera walking on El Morro in Puerto Rico, and John Coltrane playing alto sax enveloped by clouds of smoke that were penetrated by the lights, Omar also had one of Charlie Brown falling after Lucy had pulled the football away.

"Here's your water, Mari." whispered Omar, not wanting the volume to spoil this moment.

She took it drank from the glass, then gave it back to him. She moved her hips back then made a pocket for him to sit down, right in the middle of her.

"Charlie Brown for a grown man?" Marisol said, as she pointed at the famous symbol of hard luck for boys all over the world.

"Yeah it helps keep me true to my music. I didn't realize it as a kid but those are tremendous Jazz pieces. Check it out next time they come on TV."

"Mari this may sound crazy but I kind of wanted to be your first one," said Omar.

Omar's playing into a ridiculous and impossible double standard infuriated her, but she supressed that feeling, and promised herself that this conversation would be had at another time. For now, all she did was point at the box of trojans and said, "This coming from such a busy man?"

"I did say it sounds crazy, and I know the whole thing is messed up. Tell me Mari, why the very pleasant surprise. Why did you want to come over?"

"You know I like you. It's no surprise."

"Why today? That's what I mean. You got a lot on your mind don't you?"

Marisol sat up, her back on the headboard. His question initiated the inevitable slow retreat from each other that happens between a couple after having made love. Sensing this Omar moved up and put his arm around her. Feeling the comfort, she slid into his side.

"It's this stuff at home and some other things…" she answered.

"You mean between Miguel Angel and your mom?"

"I try to stay out of it but"

"Your mom needs to realize that Migue is a going to go ahead with his plans, right or wrong. Besides, that cat Big Angel isn't all that bad. My cousin tells me that when Big Angel hires his band for his parties, he always pays them right after they finish playing the last song. He's all business, no messing around."

They both looked out of the open window and saw that it was dark and the streetlights were on. They could hear the sound of the ice cream truck coming from down the street. They took in this peaceful scene for a moment before continuing a conversation that had the potential to pull them in different directions.

"You don't know all the things that go on in his business. Men have been killed at his place." said Marisol.

"But Migue won't be involved in that."

"I know my brother can handle himself, but my mother is only doing what she has been doing from the time he was a little boy and that is protecting him from any danger. Even if Migue knows what's up, Big Angel's shop can be a dangerous place."

Omar leaned in to give her a kiss. He took hold of her upper lip with his and the sound of their mouths coming together was a momentary respite from reality. They understood that Miguel Angel was taking the risk of being around illegal situations that could harm you in order to live life as a human being with dignity. They also realized that Miguel Angel like so many others, had learned how to navigate this treacherous sea.

"You mentioned something about other things" said Omar.

"Other things?"

"Yeah some other things on your mind that brought you here."

Marisol went on to tell him how she hadn't seen Valentina for weeks, and with the news of the independendistas getting killed at the armory, she was extremely worried for her. She told him about how her friendship with Valentina had given her the courage to start sharing her poetry with an audience and also to explore the world confidently as a Puerto Rican woman. Mrs. Marlowe watered the seed that Sonia had been and now it was Valentina that assured her she was ready to share all of her talents.

This natural progression of conversation then led to Marisol telling Omar that she was going to UCLA in the fall and was thinking about staying in California. Her plans did not coincide with his going back to New York and the recording opportunities that were waiting for him. Hearing this hurt Omar. As a man raised and taught to be a Casanova, he was much more comfortable with breaking hearts.

"Look Mari. You have to be careful with people like Valentina," he said not wanting to talk about losing her anymore.

"What? What do you mean?" asked Marisol, as she was puzzled by the look on his face. He had gone from being comforting and supportive to looking defensive.

"Sometimes they'll tell you anything to win you over," said Omar.

"Like my poetry isn't any good, or like I don't belong at a university like UCLA?" Marisol stood up, put her bra back on, then the rest of her clothes following in quick succession.

"First that stupid ass remark about me not being a virgin. Like what was I supposed to say, 'yes, take me Omar, I've been waiting for you to give it up to you.' And now this, you trying to keep me down or what?"

"Calm down, Mari. I didn't say all that. It's just that I thought it would be really cool if you came to check out New York with me. I know you'd love it." Omar took her hand and kissed it.

"Get those messed up ideas out of your head, then come talk to me," said Marisol.

She got the rest of her belongings and left.

CHAPTER 10

*T*hree days had passed and after not finding Valentina at home, Marisol returned to the Cultural Center hoping to hear some good news about her from Mr. Sanchez. However, this visit left her even more shaken than the last one. He had not heard from her and by the nonchalant way in which he talked about Valentina, Marisol got the impression that he didn't care. It was almost as if in his eyes, Valentina had become a lost cause, a liability instead of a valuable rebel. The revolution had no place for a useless junkie. He then revealed to Marisol that Valentina was probably strung out on dope, who knows where.

Marisol did not care about Valentina the soldier. Her heart was focused on finding the human being who for her had been a lighthouse in her journey of self love and acceptance. From the deep, unknown parts of her mind Marisol remembered all of the places in the neighborhood, that for good reason had been set off limits by her mother.

One of these places was only a block away from the same park in which children innocently played, not knowing that in the near future one of them would find themselves strung out in a dark hallway of this wretched building.

Marisol hadn't even thought about asking Omar or Miguel Angel to go with her, but she knew that it was dangerous and that she should not go alone. The one person who immediately accepted her request and accompanied her was Father Alberto. Father Alberto did not hesitate when she asked. After his time in El Salvador dealing with both righteous and corrupt people, he believed in doing anything he could to make people whole again. And he was fond of Valentina because he knew that the liberation that she was seeking for Puerto Rico was so intricately tied to her existence as a full and dignified human being. Valentina and Father Alberto shared the ability to profoundly feel hypocrisy and calculated cruelty.

As Marisol and Father Alberto approached a three story building, they saw that the doors were open. For many years community groups had wanted this place closed and condemned. The current occupants had ripped through the city's orange signs and took out the wooden boards in order to gain access to a place where they could inject relief into their veins, in the form of liquid death.

Marisol's heart became a giant pounding drum, but she steadied herself enough to pull the door, which creaked open. She gagged and almost threw up from the smell of urine and feces that hit her the second that they walked into the first apartment. In the corner of what was once a living room she could make out two men. One was holding a spoon while the other dropped in the brown packet of powder.

A rat scurried across the floor, and Marisol didn't even flinch. Under any other circumstance she would have run right out of the building, but she had to find Valentina. They continued looking, being careful not to touch or interrupt any of the addicts from getting their fix.

There was no sign of Valentina on the first floor so they decided to go up to the second floor. Out of intuition Marisol walked diagonally to her left towards a woman who was sitting in a corner nearly passed out, and her head in between her knees. Father Alberto gently tugged her arm reminding her to be careful. When Marisol got to the woman she touched her hair, which was dripping with sweat.

"Uuuuuh," moaned the woman. She looked up, her eyes rolled inside of her head.

"Valentina it's you!" Marisol started crying from joy and the shock of seeing Valentina like this.

Father Alberto walked over and said a prayer filled with gratitude and anger. Together, they lifted Valentina up and they were able to walk her out of this wretched place. Valentina did not offer any resistance when the three of them got into Father Alberto's car.

However, Valentina stated screaming, once they arrived at Doña Aurora's unofficial cold turkey clinic. Here, she cursed Marisol. Still, determined to go through hell with her friend, Marisol didn't give up.

Once inside Valentina was so exhausted she fell asleep in bed, Marisol and Doña Aurora stayed on the other side of the locked door. Doña Aurora then asked Marisol to come with her to the kitchen and help prepare the broth.

When they came back from the kitchen, they could hear Valentina screaming in agony. Her muscles were in a tight knot and she began to vomit uncontrollably. After waiting what seemed like a lifetime, Doña Aurora unlocked the door. Marisol ran and put her arms around Valentina, who was curled up in a ball and shaking. This continued for three days. When Marisol wasn't feeding Valentina, she was helping Doña Aurora wash the bed sheets and scrub the vomit off of the walls.

After a week of dedicating herself to Valentina's recovery. Marisol came home one evening and found Sonia eating alone.

"Sit. I will get you a plate," said Sonia. Marisol had called her during the time that she was fighting and crying alongside Valentina. But this did not stop Sonia from being angry with Marisol. Sonia suppressed this because of everything happening with Miguel Angel and more importantly she saw that Marisol was exhausted and hungry.

"No mami. I just want to go to bed," answered Marisol.

"Please, Mari. Sit. You look so tired. After a week at Doña Aurora's, I know that you were probably too busy and worried to eat right."

"How do you know about what goes on there?"

"Don't you know how many mothers in this neighborhood have had their sons at that place? Everyone at church knows that is where addicts are taken to get clean."

"Thank God for Father Alberto," said Marisol.

"Another nut. Sit down. I'll be right back with the arroz con gandules y bistec," said Sonia as she stood up and gently guided Marisol by her shoulders to a chair.

Sonia went in to the kitchen and turned on the stove. She placed a pot of rice on it and stirred it to make sure that it reheated evenly. Then she took out pieces of steak, added a lilt bit of water and put them in the frying pan. She started humming a melody, even during these difficult moments that left her feeling drained, she felt so much joy in preparing food for Miguel Angel and Marisol.

Feeling exhausted and her muscles aching, Marisol did not want to be there waiting for Sonia to come back. Her head was a boulder falling on to the table. She was asleep for only a few minutes.

"Here you are. Mari. Wake up." Sonia put the plate down and sat next to Marisol.

"You need to eat. This is what you get for getting involved with that crazy girl," said Sonia to a Marisol who was coming in and out of sleep and trying her best to not lose her temper with her mother. She did not want to be disrespectful.

"Mom I...."

"I knew that girl was trouble," Sonia interrupted.

With that Marisol snapped.

"No. You're the problem!" screamed Marisol.

Her mother's judgement of Valentina sent a bolt of electricity through her body and in one motion she got up and threw the food on the floor, smashing the plate in tiny pieces.

"I told you I was tired, but you just keep pushing and pushing, and pushing. At least Valentina isn't a hypocrite like you," continued Marisol.

"Hypocrite? What do you mean?" asked Sonia.

"You keep telling Miguel Angel to stay away from Big Angel and then the other night you go out with him?"

"I did that to protect your brother and I do the same for you. I will fight for you both until the day I die." Sonia's voice cracked as tears started coming down her face.

"Well don't protect me and mind your own business." Marisol turned her back to Sonia, walked to her bedroom and slammed the door.

Sonia did not follow her. Instead she got a broom and dustpan and started cleaning up the pieces of china and food that were on the floor.

"Hey, kid." Oscar called Miguel Angel who was underneath the hood of a car, in front of Mrs. Larsen's garage.

"What's up?" answered Miguel Angel.

"Big Angel wants to see you tonight at seven, his place."

"Going out tonight, man." Miguel Angel stood up, took a rag, wiped the oil from the dip stick, and put it back in the engine without looking at Oscar.

"Seven tonight. Just be there, kid." With that Oscar got back in his car and drove away.

Miguel Angel had a date with Dolores at the Blue Garden Chinese restaurant. They had met at one of his drag races.

After receiving the message from Oscar, Miguel Angel finished the oil change and left earlier than usual, giving him enough time to go home and get ready for his date. He figured that his meeting with Big Angel wouldn't take long.

When Miguel Angel got to Big Angel's office, he looked at his nails while waiting for Big Angel to come in. He was happy that there wasn't any dirt or grease on them. Following Omar's advice, he tried looking clean and sharp all of the time. He picked up a small mirror from Big Angel's desk and patted his hair to make sure that none of it was out of place.

Big Angel walked in and looked at Miguel Angel.

"You look good, kid," he said.

"Hooking up with a real pretty girl tonight" said Miguel Angel with confidence.

"Remember what I told you the other night, kid?"

"When?"

"The night I dropped off your mom. I told you no more racing. Remember?"

The unspoken anger coming from both of them created a tension that had never been present in any conversation between them.

"You and mami together was weird, man," said Miguel Angel.

"Don't worry. Your mom was just looking out for you. That's why she was with me," said Big Angel.

This was the first time that Big Angel had had to explain any of his actions to Miguel Angel.

Smiling, Miguel Angel sat down in the chair at the desk while Big Angel was still standing.

"So you stopped racing, right, kid?" asked Big Angel as he walked over and stood right in front of Miguel Angel.

"Yeah, everything's cool, Big Angel."

Big Angel then grabbed Miguel Angel by the collar with both hands and pulled him right up to his face.

Suddenly, Miguel Angel's new found confidence and cool was completely gone. He had never seen Big Angel's cold, lifeless expression directed right at him. Big Angel pulled Miguel Angel in closer, looked right into his eyes, and spoke in a chilling almost whisper.

"Don't lie to me. They saw you two nights ago at the race on Clybourn. Do you want to crash and die or end up with a million broken bones in the hospital?"

Miguel Angel started crying. He slid down back into the chair as Big Angel let him go.

"Kid, you know that I would never hurt you"

"Then why did you grab me like that?"

"I don't what you to end up like those poor bastards. Dead, or worse, vegetables because they want to win a lousy hundred bucks on a stupid drag race. You're gonna make more money working for me, kid. Understand?

Big Angel grabbed him by the chin and then finished cleaning up Miguel Angel's face with his handkerchief.

"Now, I mean it. No more racing. Haven't I always looked out for you?"

"Yeah." Miguel Angel nodded as he straightened out his shirt.

"Where are you meeting this lucky girl?" asked Big Angel.

"Chinese place, the Blue Garden."

"Here, dessert's on me. Show her a good time and get lucky."

Big Angel handed Miguel Angel a twenty dollar bill and hugged him.

Oscar came in interrupting. "Hey, Big Angel. Conglese's guys are downstairs getting out of their cars. Sorry."

"That's alright Migue is off to his hot date at the Blue Garden. Don't spill any soy sauce on that nice shirt, kid," said Big Angel as he sat down at his desk, and opened the drawer to make sure that his revolver was right where he needed it to be.

Miguel Angel said goodbye and nodded to Oscar. He noticed that Oscar closed the door behind him and Big Angel started looking at his ledger with Oscar right over him.

Two days later, Miguel Angel and Omar met at the park. Both baseball diamonds were full with little league players who walked up to the batter's box, took off their helmets, wiped the sweat from their forehead, then made the sign of the cross before lifting their bats and squarely facing the pitcher. They didn't do this out of Catholic devotion. They carried out this ritual because they wanted to be just like Clemente or the Alou brothers. When they did connect with a pitch, you could hear the crack of the bat and the players on the bench jumping up and down, cheering.

With the exception of two clumsy boys playing a game of one on one, the basketball courts were empty. The more skilled players would come out later when the sun was about to go down.

"Paradise tonight, right?" said Miguel Angel as he leaned back against the bench, taking a sip from his favorite piragua de coco.

"Don't know, man. We played until two in the morning last night." Omar answered him looking down at the grass. He bent over, picked up a daisy and started plucking it while silently reciting, "she loves me, she loves me not."

"It's going to be packed with ladies, man"

"What's up with that girl that you took to the Blue Garden Migue?"

Miguel Angel took a moment to wave at a car that had stopped. The driver turned down the music of Hector Lavoe's 'El Todopoderoso' and honked his horn.

"Hold up, I'll be right back," said Miguel Angel. He walked to the car and had a brief conversation with the driver, then went back to the bench.

"Who was that?" asked Omar.

"Mark. He's alright. Wants me to check out his muffler," answered Miguel Angel.

"Isn't that the guy who runs those after midnight drag races?"

"Yeah but I ain't doing that no more." For a brief second, Miguel Angel thought about his last meeting with Big Angel and the fear he felt seeing Big Angel as a menacing threat, came over him. "Like I was saying, I...... I...... damn! I forgot what I was going to say."

"We were talking about your date at the Chinese place the other night," said Omar to Miguel.

"It was cool," replied Miguel Angel as he winked at Omar. "But this is tonight." He raised his hand, and they gave each other five.

"I'm thinking about maybe hooking up with Mari tonight," said Omar.

"End of convo man. I don't want to know nothing about that. That's between you and her." Miguel Angel hit the bottom of the piragua to make sure that he got all of the crushed ice. He drank what was left and went to throw the rest away.

"Besides, Mari is going to be taking care of Valentina tonight," said Miguel Angel.

Later that evening Marisol was with Valentina. Valentina was slowly making her way back, putting together the scattered fragments of her life.

"Thanks for making this" said Valentina as she sipped Sonia's chicken soup.

"Mami did. It's her way of making the pain go away" answered Marisol, thinking about how Sonia did not continue the argument the morning after Marisol smashed her dinner and plate on the floor.

110

Marisol sat at the edge of Valentina's bed, just looking at her then said, "Why Valentina?"

"Why what?"

"You know." Marisol did not want to be judgmental but she needed to know how someone so vibrant and loving could inflict so much pain on herself. "Why do you do this to yourself? You know so much about our people, history, relationships. I mean you helped me come alive and dared me to be brave with my art, my poetry. I don't get it."

Valentina started talking and with each word that she uttered her voice became louder. "That's exactly why Mari. I see everything, the violence, brutality, undeclared war to keep people poor, greed, all kinds of people chasing after money and drunk on power. I'm not just talking about rich people or the government. When does it end Mari?" A tear rolled down her cheek, then more tears flowed. "And every time I start putting that poison in my veins, I say that it's going to be the last time. But at least my mind is turned off, and it doesn't hurt Mari. It doesn't hurt anymore."

Marisol pulled on Valentina's shoulder and sat her up, putting her arms around her, and together they cried in silence.

That same night Sonia found herself sitting in front of her window, sipping on a cup of homemade rum that Lucy had given her at Christmas. It was hot, and people were waiting for the rain to cool them off. They were outside in front of their buildings fanning themselves. Some were drinking beer, others soda but they all knew that in a few months that brutal winter would be back. So they took advantage of being out in the warmth of summer.

Sonia was an eagle high on a mountain, waiting for the last man to come out of Big Angel's garage. Once that happened she would find him alone and kill him. It had seemed like years since she had bought the gun from Fast Frankie, and now she was ready to use it. She did not want it to come to this, but in her eyes she had no choice.

She saw a man in a suit jacket with his collar turned up and his pants pockets literally turned inside out and sobbing, but with enough balance and awareness to hail a cab. Sonia thought that he must have been another fool who had lost his money gambling at Big Angel's place. She wondered if the man had a family, and how many bills would go unpaid as a result of his foolishness.

She felt the gun in her purse, and then took another drink. Her eyelids became heavier with each passing second, and each time hat her head snapped back, it did so with more force. The glass fell from her hand and her drink spilled on her dress.

She didn't notice because at that moment she was dreaming that she was back in Puerto Rico at age fourteen, in her parents' backyard. The sound of horses trotting, and the smell of the fresh vegetation contrasted with the blasts coming from the gun she was holding. Her father stood behind her and made sure that her arm and aim were straight. He congratulated her for hitting three of the six bottles.

Her mother couldn't believe that he was teaching their daughter this deadly art. But she also knew that she did not want Sonia to be assaulted at the store on the days when she would be working there alone, while her husband went to the next town for wholesale goods.

Suddenly Sonia was awakened by the sound of three loud shots that once again came from Big Angel's garage. The ambulance and police cars came speeding down the street with their sirens blasting.

She started rubbing her face, trying to wake up, and looked at the clock to realize that she had been asleep for a half hour. In a moment of irrational fear she ran to her bedroom and hid the gun inside a pair of winter boots. Noticing the wet stains on her dress, she took another dress from her closet, went to the bathroom and splashed cold water on her face.

Neighbors, visitors and strangers had formed a circle of curious people around the building, there to see the latest violent spectacle. The paramedics came out of the garage carrying a body covered by a white sheet. Sonia immediately knew that it was Big Angel by his shoes and his hand that was dangling from the stretcher.

Sonia started weeping, simultaneously feeling sorrow and relief. Big Angel was dead, and now her son would be safe.

Later that night it rained. Those who had been out on the block playing congas, exchanging the latest gossip, or instigating a fight between two friends who had had a few too many beers, all went inside for cover.

Miguel Angel and Omar were on the north side of town at Club Paradise. Omar was in a booth looking at his drink, mindlessly stirring it with the straw. He didn't care about all the beautiful women around him. His only thought was of Marisol.

The dance floor was packed with couples moving to the rhythm of Donna Summers sensuously singing, "I Feel Love". A disco globe spinning on the ceiling combined with strobe lights made everyone a great dancer. In the middle of all of this was Miguel Angel dancing with his arms around a woman named Valerie. She had his back to him, and he softly kissed her neck.

The music then changed to the beat of Barry White's, 'It's Ecstasy When You Lay Down Next to Me." The slightly slower tempo gave Miguel Angel and Valerie a chance to sit down and they walked with their arms around each other to where Omar was sitting.

"Be right back baby. Order me a double vodka," said Valerie into Miguel Angel's ear before going off to the ladies' room.

"Whew! She got a lot of energy man. I'm thirsty," said Miguel Angel. He motioned to a waitress.

"Rum and Coke?" she asked.

"That's right, and a double vodka," asked Miguel Angel. "What about you Omar?"

"I'm cool. Maybe you should slow down too Migue."

"Hell no! This is Paradise, baby. We're here to speed up!"

The waitress went to get the drinks and Miguel Angel scanned the dance floor and the rest of the club.

"You looking for Plan B?" asked Omar.

"You never know, man. You never know," replied Miguel Angel. "Look, man, I'm leaving in a little bit, but I can't take you back."

"Aw, come on, man. How am I supposed to get home?" said Omar.

"Bus, cab, come on, man, figure it out. You want some money?"

"No. I'm good Migue."

A few minutes later the waitress came back with the drinks and Miguel Angel took out a wad of cash giving her a generous tip.

Valerie came back to the booth. She quickly wiped her nose with her bare hand, making sure that there wasn't any residue. She then turned Miguel Angel's face to her and they passionately started kissing.

"Finish your drink, baby. It's time to take me home." Valerie took her double shot of vodka. Then Omar watched Miguel Angel and Valerie walk out of the club holding hands.

The rain that had been falling all night had let up a bit. Miguel Angel and Valerie found the drops of water falling from the night sky to be refreshing after their night of extended foreplay on the dance floor. They laughed and skipped over some of the puddles crossing the street to the car. Being the perfect gentleman, Miguel Angel walked over to Valerie's side and opened her door.

"Just take Lake Shore down to Fullerton, honey," said Valerie.

"Got it," said Miguel Angel, closing the door for her.

Miguel Angel drove to the stop light. While they were waiting, a car with a man who had had one too many drinks drove up to the passenger side. He looked at Valerie, threw her a kiss and started revving up the engine.

"He wants to race, baby," said Valerie as she rubbed Miguel Angel's knee with her hand.

"It's slippery." Even though this wasn't the drag races prohibited to him, Miguel Angel did not want to defy Big Angel, but he told himself he was a man, not a little kid.

"It's only two blocks to the Foster entrance, and you do want me to stay hot don't you, baby?" said Valerie.

With that, Miguel Angel made up his mind. The light changed to green, and both drivers stepped on the gas. Miguel Angel jumped out in front. Suddenly, as they were about to cross the first intersection, a speeding car came out from nowhere and crashed right into them. Miguel Angel tried slamming on the brakes to avoid hitting other cars, causing them to flip over.

A janitor who had finished his shift and was waiting at a bus stop ran to a pay phone and called 911.

When the ambulance arrived, they pulled Miguel Angel and Valerie out of the car.

"This one is still alive", said a paramedic as he pressed Valerie's neck for signs of a pulse.

"Not so lucky for this one," said his partner as he spread a white sheet over Miguel Angel's dead body.

CHAPTER 11

*H*olding back tears, Father Alberto spoke the last words of his eulogy for another senseless death of a young Puerto Rican man in this beautiful, yet at times unforgiving, city. Miguel Angel should have been preparing to live his life to the fullest.

Sonia looked around the room of the Rios funeral home. She had on the same type of black dress that she wore to the service for Rafael's wake. She stood in front of his coffin and searched for the eyes that would never again pierce her soul. Never again would she hear his voice calling, "Mami, Mami." These memories felt torturous and did not console her at all.

She walked over to the floral arrangements and read a card from his old school, sent by his former social worker Mr. Young. This touched her heart.

Sonia felt a hand on her shoulder and she turned to see that it was Omar crying.

"I loved him," said Omar.

"We all did," was all Sonia could say.

"It's all my fault Sra. Concepción."

Sonia held his arms then started drying his tears with her hands pressing softly against his cheeks.

"Miguel Angel was going to do what he wanted. Don't blame yourself."

Sonia hugged Omar while looking at Father Alberto, who was drinking water from a paper cup, and talking to the owner of the funeral home, Juan Rios. She saw this as the opportunity that she had been waiting for and told Omar that although they would miss Miguel Angel for the rest of their lives, the pain would be a little less with each passing day. She didn't believe her own lie, but it was the only way she knew to comfort Omar and relieve him of his guilt. She then made her way to Father Alberto.

"Sr. Rios, can we please use your office? The priest and I need to speak," asked Sonia.

"Claro que sí Sra. Concepción," answered Mr. Rios.

Sonia and Father Alberto silently walked back to the office and Mr. Rios opened the door, telling them to take as long as they needed.

Sonia made no effort to hide the anger in her eyes. Father Alberto asked if she would like to sit down. But she preferred standing so she could let out what she had been holding in for the past week.

"Why, Father Alberto? Damn it, why?!, cried Sonia as she walked over to Mr. Rios desk and pounded her clenched fist on it.

"God feels your pain, Sonia." Father Alberto truly believed this, but after seeing so many people gunned down by death squads in El Salvador, and consoling mothers of young 14 year old gang members who had been shot down in broad daylight in the streets of this city, he had the same question and doubts as Sonia.

"God! What God?" Sonia continued. "The God who lets so many people starve to death? Soldiers kill in his name, in his name, Father Alberto." She grabbed him by his collar wanting to rip it out but he gently stopped her and she took a moment to compose herself.

"I have always followed his way, Father. I learned the rosary and prayed at baptisms and funerals. Even when Miguel Angel and Marisol's father was killed, I saw it as God's will and worked hard to raise my children on my own. I kept going to church, sent them to catechism, made sure they did their first communion and confirmation, and for what? For what?" Sonia slumped down on a chair and started crying, her entire body moving with the waves of her grief.

Father Alberto knelt in front of her, put his hand on her shoulder and started crying with her.

"I don't know why, Sonia. I don't know."

And they continued consoling each other in their pain hoping that this would give them enough strength to keep their faith.

Marisol and Sonia started drinking their coffee, after having had their eggs with a Kaiser roll, that Marisol had gotten from the bakery. They had started to get back into the routines that reminded them of moments when there were storms around them but they still found the time to start the day together as a triumphant trio. As children both Miguel Angel and Marisol knew that Sonia would guide and make them strong enough to face indifferent teachers, schoolyard bullies, and any person who would try to take away their dignity. Breakfast for them was the ritual they needed to start the day, and they continued it even now that Miguel Angel was gone.

It had been a month since Miguel Angel's place at the table sat empty. Sonia had stopped setting three plates. She found that the realization that her son was dead came in small stages, with each one hurting as much as the first one, until with time they collectively hurt just a little less.

"Are you ready to go back to work, Mami?" asked Marisol.

"Yes and no. I have to go back because Mr. Reynolds can't hold my job forever. But I don't know. Sometimes I think that I'll go crazy in this house all day, but I really don't want to hear people talking about business, write reports, or take phone calls" answered Sonia.

"You need to be there," said Marisol.

Marisol had on a blue blouse and jeans. She sat with poise and was becoming more confident each day. She was writing in her journal in which she had captured moments of lovers kissing on the sidewalk with their arms at their side, not needing to hold each other to stay together in the same space; of a French couple walking up the stairs of the Art Institute; and three German girls were pointing to Michigan Avenue, on the way to explore more of the city. These were the some of the places and people that Marisol drew from as she kept expanding her poetic horizons.

"I am so proud of you, mija. In two weeks you will be going away to school" said Sonia.

Marisol looked at her thinking that she didn't want to leave Sonia alone at this time.

"I will be fine," said Sonia, not wanting to get in the way of her daughter's chosen path.

"Poor Omar. How is he?" Sonia asked playfully, changing the subject but wanting to know about the state of their relationship and how Marisol felt about him.

"Don't worry. Omar is more than fine. He's playing and recording with some of the best bands in New York," answered Marisol. "We are thinking about maybe getting together over Christmas."

This brought Sonia a bit of consolation. She wanted to experience complete joy for her daughter without feeling the loss of her son. Perhaps she would never get to that place.

Sonia placed her hand across the table cloth at the exact place where Miguel Angel would have sat and then started picking up the plates to take them back to the kitchen.

"Are you coming to hear me at the Cultural Center tonight, Mami?" asked Marisol.

"Of course, mija. Why would you even ask?"

Three poets were reading this night and there was going to be a Bomba dance segment before the last poet, who on this evening happened to be Marisol.

That day at work Sonia was almost robotic as she answered phone calls, took memos, and handled files. At lunch she hardly said a word to anybody as she ate a salami and cheese sandwich with a cup of coffee. When five o'clock came around, she just waved goodbye to Mr. Reynolds, walked to the street, and took the two buses to the Betances Cultural Center.

She arrived at the door and was immediately hugged by Valentina. Sonia noticed the loss of weight from Valentina's latest bout with addiction but was happy to hear about Valentina's plans to go live on a small farm with her uncle in Hatillo, Puerto Rico.

Sonia sat next to Valentina and watched the musicians playing Bomba and Plena as the people in the audience sang along. She was asked to dance but she was not emotionally ready for that. She was only there to support Marisol.

Once the music was over, it came time for Marisol.

The host called her on to the stage. Marisol just looked directly at the back wall not wanting to focus on anyone. She cleared her throat, took a sip of water and began reciting her poem.

> I write to express who I am, what I feel, and to tell the world I have gone from being a girl to asserting who I am as a woman. Breaking chains in my mind I didn't even know were there. I am no longer a shy, meek child afraid to ask a kind Polish lady for sweet chocolate long johns, Kaiser rolls, and cherry cheese danish. "Speak up honey"
>
> I would hear; "Girl you got that pelo malo. You gotta relax it." Relax yourself I said in my mind. But today I say it out loud. No more wearing wool caps on a hot summer day to hide my reddish brown hair that likes me to be tamed. Today, I will curl it, cut it, loose, tight, so many styles and the choices are mine, all mine.
>
> Mami and Papi teach me all about Borinquen Bella. But not about the palm trees and sugar cane that turned into snow when you got off the plane. Dance to Tito Rodriguez, Maelo and Cortijo and hold each other tight as La Lupe casts a powerful enchanting spell. From a never ending well of despair and happiness you make each other strong.

And you my beautiful sister who I first saw stopping people on the street. Some smiled, some stopped but most did not want to talk to the bold independentista with the red scarf around her afro. But you my dear friend saw in me what I was afraid to be. You watered the seed planted in me and showed there is everything right in being free.

I am no longer afraid. Today I make love on top, yes on top. Can you dig it baby or does that take away your masculinity? If it does it is not my concern for I am here to learn with each passing minute more and more about myself and this world. What saddens me is that a part of my holy trinity, is no longer here to hear my new song.

If you can hear me from wherever you are brother, I love you. I love myself, my skin, my hair, my body, my soul, my mind. Yes every single part of me. For who are they to put me down and have the audacity within their pomposity to call me lazy? No I am not crazy.

We are a beautiful people and are already free. Free in our mind and the land will come with time.

Mami you gave me life and with these words I show love and gratitude.

Because you were the first to show me that, we
are a beautiful people and are already free. Free
in our mind and the land will come with time.

She finished and the room stayed silent. Valentina stood up
started clapping and the rest of the audience joined in the standing
ovation.

Marisol's eyes were only focused on Sonia. Marisol and Sonia
embraced, laughed and cried with a joy and grief that only they
could understand.

Printed in the United States
by Baker & Taylor Publisher Services